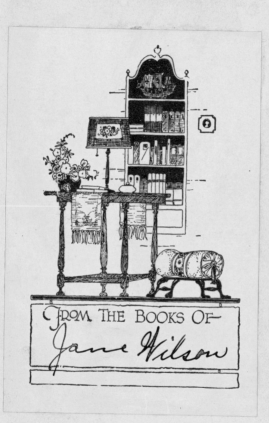

FROM THE BOOKS OF

Jane Wilson

Leila claimed the privilege of conveying the freshman to Silverton Hall, her destination.
(Marjorie Dean, College Sophomore) Page 115

MARJORIE DEAN
COLLEGE SOPHOMORE

By PAULINE LESTER

Author of

"Marjorie Dean, College Freshman," "Marjorie Dean,
College Junior," "Marjorie Dean, College Senior,"
and
The Marjorie Dean High School Series

A. L. BURT COMPANY
Publishers   New York

THE
Marjorie Dean College Series

A Series of Stories for Girls 12 to 18 Years of Age

By PAULINE LESTER

Marjorie Dean, College Freshman
Marjorie Dean, College Sophomore
Marjorie Dean, College Junior
Marjorie Dean, College Senior

MARJORIE DEAN, COLLEGE SOPHOMORE

CHAPTER I

THE RETURN.

"HAMILTON, at last!" Marjorie Dean's utterance expressed her satisfaction of the journey's near end.

"Yes; Hamilton, at last," repeated Muriel Harding. "This September it doesn't matter a particle whether or not we are met at the station. We are sophomores. We know what to do and where to go without the help of the celebrated Sans Soucians." Muriel's inflection was one of sarcasm.

"All the help they ever gave us as freshmen can be told in two words: *no help*. Forget the Sans. I hate to think of them. I hope not one of them is back. The station platform will look beautiful without them." Jerry Macy delivered herself of this uncomplimentary opinion as she began methodically to gather up her luggage.

"How very sad to see two Hamiltonites so utterly lacking in college spirit." Veronica Lynne simulated pained surprise.

"Yes; isn't it?" retorted Jerry. "Whose fault is it that Muriel and I haven't last year's trusting faith in reception committees? Recall how we stood on the station platform like a flock of dummies with no one to bid us the time of day or say a kind word to us. No wonder my love for the Sans is a minus quantity."

"You aren't following your own advice," calmly criticized Lucy Warner. "You said 'Forget the Sans' and went right on talking about them."

"'And thou, too, Brutus!'" Jerry dramatically struck her hand to her forehead. "It is getting to the point where one can't say a single word around here without being called to account for it. This distressing state of affairs must stop." She frowned portentously at Lucy, who merely giggled. "You may blame Ronny for egging me on to further cutting remarks about the Sans. I was prepared to forget them until she undertook to call Muriel and I down. Then I simply had to defend our position."

"What position?" innocently queried Ronny. "I was not aware that you and Muriel——"

"The train has stopped. Didn't you know it?" was Marjorie's amused interruption. "Stop squabbling and come along." She was already in the

aisle and impatient to be on the move. "Helen
Trent is out on the platform, Jeremiah. I just
caught a glimpse of her. I hope Leila and Vera are
out there, too. Let me assist you into the aisle."
Marjorie playfully gripped Jerry's arm in a vain
effort to draw her to her feet.

"Thank you. I can assist myself. I am not yet
aged enough to require your services. You may
carry my suitcase, if you like. It's as heavy as
lead."

"Charmed, but unfortunately I have one to carry
equally heavy," Marjorie hastily declined. "I only
offered to haul you up from the seat. My offer
didn't include luggage carrying."

"You are a fake." Jerry rose and prepared to
follow Marjorie down the aisle. As she went she
peered anxiously out of the car windows for a first
glimpse of her particular friend, Helen Trent.

The eyes of the other four Lookouts were also
turned eagerly toward the station platform in search
of their Hamilton friends.

A year had elapsed since first the Five Travelers,
as the quintette of Sanford girls had named themselves, had set foot in the Country of College. Each
was recalling now how very strangely she had felt
on first glimpsing Hamilton station with its bevy
of laughing, chatting girls, not one of whom they
knew. Then they had been entering freshmen,

with everything to learn about college. Now they were sophomores, with a year of college experience to their credit. What befell Marjorie Dean and her four Lookout chums as freshmen at Hamilton College has already been recounted in "MARJORIE DEAN, COLLEGE FRESHMAN."

"Hooray!" rejoiced Jerry, from the top step of the train, waving her handbag, a magazine and a tennis racket, all of which she clutched in her right hand. This vociferous greeting was for Helen, who was making equally vociferous signals of jubilation at the descending travelers.

Marjorie had also caught sight of Leila Harper and Vera Mason, and was waving them a welcome. Lucy's eyes were fixed on Katherine Langly, whom she knew had come down to the station especially to meet her. Veronica and Muriel were exchanging gay hand salutations with a group of Silverton Hall girls prior to greeting them on the platform. An instant and the Five Travelers were free of the train and surrounded.

"And is it yourself?" Leila Harper was hugging Marjorie in an excess of true Irish affection. "Vera had a hunch this morning that you would be here today. I said it was too early; that you wouldn't be here until the first of next week. She would have it her way, so we drove down to meet this train. Now I know she has the gifted eye and the seeing mind, as we Irish say."

"It is a good thing for us that she had that hunch," declared Marjorie, turning to Vera and holding out both hands. "I was hoping you would both be here to meet us. I would have wired you, Leila, but was not sure that you would be back at Hamilton so early. We are here a week earlier than last year. We wanted to be at home as long as we could, but we felt that, as sophomores, we ought to come back earlier to help the freshies. We had such a lonesome time on our freshman appearance at Hamilton, you know."

"Yes, I know," returned Leila significantly. "That was one of the Sans' performances which was never explained. Away with them. This is no time to think of them. The rest of your Lookouts are running off and leaving you, Beauty." This last had been Leila's pet name for Marjorie since the latter had won the title at a beauty contest given the previous year at the freshman frolic.

"They'd better not run far. I am going to take you all back to college in my car," Vera hospitably informed Marjorie. "Leila brought Helen Trent, Katherine, Ethel Laird and Martha Merrick to the station in her car. Ethel expects a freshman cousin from Troy, New York. Martha came along because she had nothing else to do. She said she would like to see if my hunch came true. She had never yet heard of one that amounted to a row of pins. She was sure you would not be on the 5.50 train. Oh, wait until I catch sight of her! She's circulating around the platform somewhere."

"So are my pals." Marjorie glanced about her, endeavoring to locate her chums. None of them were far away. Lucy and Katherine Langly were already approaching. Muriel and Ronny were still engaged with the group of Silverton Hall girls. Neither Robina Page nor Portia Graham were among them. It was quite likely they had not yet returned to Hamilton.

"Just as soon as we can collect your crowd, Marjorie, we'll spin you along to the Hall. Then, I beg to inform you, you are needed at a grand rally at Baretti's. Let us have faith in the stars that those four pals of yours have not recklessly accepted invitations to other celebrations. And if they have, I shall be in a high temper. I warn you." Leila showed her white teeth in a smile that was certainly no indication of ill-temper.

"They haven't, Leila," Marjorie happily assured. She was thinking what a joy it was to see Leila again. "On the train we all agreed not to accept any invitations to dinner on this first evening. Our plan was to take you and Vera, Helen and Katherine and Hortense Barlow to Baretti's for a feast, pro-

vided you were all here. If some of you were missing, then we thought we would take those of you
who had come back to the Colonial, and wait until
you all arrived for the other celebration. You see,
it is to be what you might call a 'first friends'' party.
Helen was the first girl we met. Now she and
Jerry are college pals. Katherine is Lucy's first
friend. Muriel is so fond of Hortense, and Ronny
and I look upon you and Vera as nearer than any
of the others. I am fond of Robin Page, and Portia
Graham, too. They really ought to be included.
Are they here, and how long have you and Vera
been back?"

Marjorie made her explanations and asked her
questions almost in the same breath.

"We have been here three days. We have been
really busy. though. We had our unpacking to do,
and we changed the furniture around in our room.
We spent one whole afternoon playing golf. We
both adore the Hamilton links. The time has gone
fast, although we have missed our own particular
cronies, especially in the evenings. Now we can
have a few jollifications before college starts."
Vera answered for Leila, who had turned to greet
Lucy Warner.

Presently Muriel and Ronny joined them, to be
warmly welcomed by the two juniors. Jerry and
Helen Trent were the last to arrive. With their

appearance among the group of staunch comrades, the entire party began a slow walk down the platform and toward the stairs which led away from the station.

"If you are in search of information as to who's where and when you may expect them, ask Helen. As I used to say of myself, 'I know everything about everybody,' I now pass on that same saying to my esteemed friend, Miss Trent." Jerry beamed on Helen with exaggerated admiration.

"Now, Jeremiah, don't you think that a rather sweeping statement? There may be just a *few* students at Hamilton I don't happen to be informed about. You will give our friends here the impression that I am a busybody. Remember I am now a junior. Try to treat me with more respect." Helen smiled indolent good nature as she thus admonished Jerry.

"I'll try, but that's all the good it will do. The whole trouble is, you don't comand my awe and respect," complained Jerry.

"Neither do you inspire such feelings in me," placidly returned Helen. "We'll simply have to go on being disrespectful to each other," she ended, with a chuckle which Jerry echoed.

"Let us see." The little company had reached the place where Leila and Vera had parked their cars. Leila now cast speculative eyes over the group. "Martha is missing. Ethel must have found her cousin, surely. If she did not find her she was to go back to the campus with us. I lost track of her after the train whistled in. Martha is probably with Ethel; helping to impress the freshman cousin with junior estate," Leila made whimsical guess. "I think we are ready to start. Nine of us; that's four to your car and five to mine, Midget."

"All right," returned Vera. "Choose your five, or, better, let your five choose you. The sooner we start, the sooner we will reach the Hall. That means a longer time to celebrate tonight."

"Delighted to ride with either of you," assured Muriel. "The main feature of this occasion is the beautiful fact that we are cherished enough to be actually met at the station and asked to ride in folks' automobiles."

"Muriel can't get over the freezing-out we met with last September," commented Ronny.

"Neither can I. I feel chilly every time I think of it. Br-r-r!" Jerry made pretense of shivering.

"Well, we all know whose fault that was," shrugged Leila.

"Precisely what I said just before we left the train," nodded Jerry. "We couldn't understand for a long time why those three Sans should have taken it upon themselves at all to meet our train. We have a clear idea now of why it was. Tonight, at the celebration, I'll hold forth on the subject. Let us not mar the sweet joy of meeting by gossiping," she ended with an irresistibly funny simper.

"No; let us not," echoed Leila dryly. "Be quick with your choosing now. Time will keep on flying."

Five minutes later, Marjorie, Ronny, Helen and Jerry were leaving the station yard in Leila's car. Muriel, Lucy, Katherine and Vera occupied the latter's smart limousine. In comparison with the subdued almost sad little party they had been on the previous September, the Five Travelers were now a very merry company of adventurers in the Country of College.

On the front seat of Leila's roadster, beside Leila, Marjorie was silent for a little, as Leila skilfully guided the trim roadster in and out of the considerable traffic of Herndon Avenue, Hamilton's main thoroughfare.

"Have you seen any of the Sans yet, Leila?" she presently questioned. The car was now turning into Highland Avenue, which led directly to Hamilton Estates. Marjorie glimpsed, in passing, the same wealth of colorful leaf and bloom she had so greatly admired when driving through the pretty town the previous autumn.

"No signs of them yet," Leila made reply. "I am

not grieving. I am wondering if they will be at the Hall again this year. Miss Remsen doesn't want them; that I know. After they made the trouble for you, she declared she would not let them come back if she could help it."

"I know." Marjorie was silent for a moment. "I had a talk with Miss Remson in June, just before college closed," she said slowly. "I asked her not to make a complaint to President Matthews on my account. I told her it would not make any difference to me if they stayed at the Hall. I did not believe it would make any to the rest of the girls. None of us had spoken to them since the meeting in the living room. None of us were in the least afraid of them. We had as much right to be at the Hall as they. She finally promised to leave me out of it entirely, but she intended to make complaint against them on her own account."

"Then they will soon be here, lug and luggage," predicted Leila with a groan. "It is the way they treated you that would have counted against them. Our president is a stickler for honor. He might readily expel them for that very performance."

"That is what I was afraid of. I should not wish a student expelled from Hamilton on my account. It was hard enough to have to call them to account, as we did last March."

"They have had all summer to get over the shock.

They'll be planning new trouble this fall." Leila spoke with the confidence of belief. "Leslie Cairns never gives up. Are you ready to fight them again, Beauty?" Leila eyed Marjorie quizzically. She asked the question in the odd, level tone she had used on first acquaintance with Marjorie.

"I think this: Our best way to fight the Sans is by influence. Their influence, founded as it is on money values, is not beneficial to Hamilton College. Ours should be founded strictly on observing the traditions of Hamilton. We must make other students see that, too. We can't lecture on the subject, of course. It will have to be a silent struggle for nobler aims. I hardly know how to explain my meaning. I only wish everyone else here had the same feeling of reverence for Hamilton that I have."

Marjorie paused, quite at a loss to put into words all that was in her heart. As they talked, the roadster had been spinning rapidly along through Hamilton Estates. Suddenly the campus, of living velvety green, appeared upon their view. The old, potent spell of its beauty gripped the little lieutenant afresh. She had a desire to rise in the seat and shout a welcome to her first Hamilton friend. A verse of a forest hymn she had learned as a child in the grade schools sprang to her memory. It was so well suited to the campus.

"I've always loved the campus, Leila," she began.
"I call it my first friend and the chimes my second.
Those two things meant the most to me when first
we came to Hamilton and felt so out of the college
picture.   Just now I happened to recall a verse of
a song we used to sing in school.   It is a hymn to
the forest, but it describes Hamilton campus and all
the college itself should stand for."   Marjorie repeated the verse, her eyes on the rolling emerald
spread:

"Who rightly scans thy beauty, a world of truth
    must read;
 Of life and hope and duty; our help in time of
    need.
 And I have read them often, those words so true
    and clear,
What heart that would not soften, thy wisdom to
    revere."

CHAPTER II.

A CELEBRATION AT BERETTI'S.

THE Lookouts' plan to entertain their friends at either Baretti's or the Colonial on their first evening at Hamilton was over-ruled by Leila and Vera. As Hortense Barlow, Robina Page and Portia Graham were still missing from their circle of friends, they agreed to postpone their own celebration until the missing ones should have returned to Hamilton. Thus Vera and Leila gained their point and were in high glee over it. Privately they were glad to have the Lookouts to themselves for the evening, with the addition only of Katherine and Helen.

The warm September day had vanished into a soft, balmy night, garnished by a full, silvery moon. The road to Baretti's was light as day and the nine girls, clad in delicate-hued summer frocks, added to the pale beauty of the night. They were in high spirits, as the incessant murmur of their voices, punctuated by frequent ripples of light laughter, amply testified.

Entering the quaint, stately restaurant, the Lookouts stopped to pay courteous respects to Guiseppe Baretti, the proud proprietor, a small, somber-eyed Italian. Their frequent patronage of Baretti's during their freshman year had made them very welcome guests. Signor Baretti's solemn face became wreathed with smiles as he greeted them.

"It is certainly good to be here again!" exclaimed Jerry. By appropriating two extra chairs from a nearby vacant table, the nine diners had managed to seat themselves without crowding at one table.

"Isn't it, though?" Vera Mason glanced happily around the circle. "I miss Baretti's dreadfully during vacations. There is really no other restaurant quite like it."

"We missed it too, this summer. Our main standby in Sanford was Sargeant's. You and Leila made its acquaintance when you were in Sanford last Easter. We used to go there so often after school. I wonder we ever had an appetite for dinner when we went home. Of course it can't be compared with Baretti's, as it is merely a confectioner's shop. We had happy times there, though," Marjorie concluded.

"It was a regular conspirator's shop," Jerry supplemented. "Whenever we had anything special to talk over, the watchword was, 'On to Sargeant's.'"

"We settled a great many weighty affairs of state

at Sargeant's." Muriel smiled reminiscently. "I
suppose Baretti's will grow dearer to us as we plod
along our college way. I like it better than the
Colonial, which lacks the air this place has. Besides, the Sans monopolize it so that I had rather
come here."

"Why did the Sans turn from Baretti's to the
Colonial?" Lucy asked tersely. Her analytic mind
had not for an instant lost sight of Vera's earlier
remark concerning the proprietor. "What happened?"

"Oh, it took a large number of straws to break
the camel's back. When it broke——"

"Bing!" obligingly supplied Jerry. "I can picture the wrath of an outraged Baretti."

"He was wrathful more than once before he said
a word. The Sans used to be awfully noisy when
they dined or lunched here. Guiseppe did not like
that. They used to reserve tables by telephone,
then, when they reached here for dinner, they would
claim he had not reserved the tables they had asked
for. That was a trick of Leslie Cairns. She would
tell him that he ought not charge extra for the tables
as he had not complied with her order properly.
There were all sorts of little points like that which
the Sans used to argue with him. They used to
tease him purposely to see him get angry. When he
is very angry he says not a word. He clenches his

hands and his face turns fiery red. His eyes snap and he looks as though he would like to turn inside out. He half opens his mouth, then turns on his heel and scuttles off.

"One evening in February," Vera continued, "Leila and I came here for dinner. One of the sophs had a birthday and she was giving a dinner to eighteen of her classmates. Remember, Leila? They had those three tables over there." Vera nodded toward the opposite side of the room. "The room was quite well filled, when in came Leslie Cairns, Joan Myers and Natalie Weyman with three girls who had come from a prep. school to spend a week-end with Joan. There wasn't a single table at which they all could sit. Instead of calling Guiseppe, Leslie Cairns walked straight to the soph who was giving the dinner, and claimed she had taken a table which Joan had reserved by telephone. The soph should simply have stayed away upon her dignity and called Signor Baretti. She was indignant, naturally, and began to argue the matter with Miss Cairns. They both grew furious and talked so loudly you could hear them all over the room. Natalie Weyman undertook to champion Leslie, and Leslie told her to shut her mouth and mind her own affairs. She is *so* uncouth when she loses her temper. Honestly, a regular pow-wow went on for a few minutes."

Vera stopped her narrative to laugh as she recalled that very stormy altercation. Leila was also laughing. Nor could the other listeners fail to be amused.

"I can imagine how that poor soph felt to be jumped on so unexpectedly, when she was playing the agreeable hostess at her own birthday party." Jerry's sympathy for the injured sophomore did not prevent her from laughing. The funny side of such tragedies invariably struck Jerry first. "How did the pow-wow end?"

"Very likely an enraged Baretti swooped down on them and read them the law in broken and indignant English," guessed Ronny, with a glance toward the cashier's desk, where the stolid little proprietor sat counting the day's receipts.

"Did he?" emphasized Vera. "He crossed the floor as though he had wings attached to his shoes. He stopped directly in front of Leslie Cairns. We couldn't hear what he said to her. It wasn't more than half a dozen sentences. They must have been strictly to the point. She glared at him and he glared back. Then she said loudly enough to be heard all over the room: 'Come on, girls. Let the dago have his hash house. I hope it burns down tonight.' The six of them went out of the restaurant, laughing. Guiseppe was wild. He swore they should never be allowed to set foot in this place again. They stayed away until after Easter. Gradually they drifted back, and he didn't reopen the quarrel. They have been on their good behavior here since then."

"Quite a collegiate performance. What?" Leila gave an exact imitation of Leslie Cairns' manner of uttering the interrogation. "Take the truth from me, our freshie year was full of just such scenes put over by those girls."

"The soph who had the fuss with Leslie Cairns is a senior this year. You may believe the Sans will get no favors from her and her party crowd. The Sans will find out some day that they can't sow tares and expect to reap flowers," concluded Vera with some warmth.

"Yes, but it will take them such a very long time to find it out," Muriel said impatiently. "If we don't stand up for the honor of our Alma Mater, who will?"

"Well, we've done some good," sturdily asserted Jerry. "We wouldn't allow the Sans to rag Katherine. The Beauty contest was an awful damper to them, especially Miss Weyman. It put a crimp in her sails. She needed to be suppressed. Then came the trouble about basket ball. The Silverton House girls deserve most of the credit for that *coup de grace*. It certainly brought the freshman class together with a snap. There are only about twelve or fifteen of the present sophs who are Sans worshippers. Miss Reid won't dare interfere with sports this year."

"A strong blow you freshies struck for fairness in college sports," commended Leila. "They will be properly managed this year."

"Miss Reid is to have only light gymnastics and folk dancing from this on," announced Helen. "There is to be a new gym instructor; a young man. He is a physical culture expert and an acrobat. He is to teach bar and trapeze work."

"You don't mean it!" Leila puckered her lips into a soft whistle. "What is to become of Miss Bailey? She is a better teacher of folk dancing than Miss Reid. Who told you, Helen?"

"Miss Bailey herself. I came up from town with her the other day in a taxi. She seems pleased with the new arrangement. She is to assist both Miss Reid and the new instructor. You know she is an athletic wonder for a woman. She does very difficult acrobatic work and understands teaching balance. That is so difficult to teach."

"Who knows? This may be Miss Reid's last year with us," Leila said with a tinge of laughing malice. "It is said a change of that kind for a teacher at college generally precedes a violent drop. If true, we must try to bear our loss. It takes time to recover from such losses. How we do ramble from the subject. Let us be turning back to our freshies' good works."

"Muriel stopped at that basket ball affair last winter," prompted Katherine. "I'll mention it before Lucy has a chance. She isn't the only one who can keep tab on things."

"I see I shall have to keep you in the background." Lucy bent a severe eye on Katherine. "You are out to steal my glory."

"Just tell her to subside, a la Leslie Cairns," suggested Helen. "What a shame that I missed that lovely party row at Baretti's. I heard echoes of it on the campus for a week afterward. Let me tell you, I admire Ronny for the way she wound up that tale the Sans started against Marjorie last March. It was the best thing that could have been done."

"Something had to be done." Ronny's gray eyes grew flinty. "Those particular girls took an unusually bold stand against her. I am surprised that they did not attempt to haze her earlier in the year."

"It probably did not occur to them," was Vera's opinion. "If it had, they might have tried it. It is strictly forbidden here. The hazers would certainly be expelled. President Matthews is down on it with both feet. A niece of his was hazed at college and contracted pneumonia. She died of it and he has been doubly opposed to it since then."

"I am glad I was saved midnight visits from sheeted ghosts or some such eerie horror," laughed Marjorie. It wouldn't have done them any good if ever they had hazed me. I would have refused to do one single thing they told me to do. It wouldn't have been a specially pleasant experience to waken suddenly and find the room inhabited by spooks. Still I wouldn't have been afraid of them. I am glad to be a soph. I am past the grind and hazing stage. Do tell the girls about Rowena Farnham, Jeremiah. You promised them you would."

"And so I will," affably consented Jerry. "I think I'll save it for dessert, though."

"I think you won't," quickly objected Leila. "Be nice and tell us now. Dessert is afar off. The sherbet and the salad stand between it."

Having come to a speedy selection of their dinner, immediately they were seated at table, they were now finishing the toothsome old-fashioned chicken pot-pie and its palatable accompaniments which was one of Baretti's most popular specialties.

"All right children, I will humor you," Jerry made gracious concession, as other protesting voices arose. "Understand this is no news to the Lookouts here assembled."

"We don't mind hearing it again. We're the pattern of amiability," Muriel made light assurance.

"Charmed, to be sure," beamed Ronny.

"I'll take your word for it." Jerry did not appear specially impressed by such overwhelming forbearance. "To begin with, the Macys spend their summers at Severn Beach. The Farnhams have a regular castle at Tanglewood, a resort about ten miles from Severn Beach. It is needless to say that Rowena and I do not exchange visits. I am happy to say I never saw her at Severn Beach. Think what the beach has been spared."

"One afternoon Hal took me to Tanglewood in his sailboat. He went to see a couple of his chums about arranging for a yacht race. I didn't care to go with him to the cottage. I knew they didn't want me butting in while they planned their race. I stayed down on the sands near the boat. Hal had promised to be back by four o'clock.

"I watched the bathers for a while. There were only a few in the water that day," Jerry continued. "Finally, I thought I would go up to a large pavilion at the head of the pier for an ice. I sat in the pavilion eating a pineapple ice as peacefully as you please. All of a sudden I realized someone had stopped beside my chair; two someones by the way. One of them was Row-ena Quarrelena Fightena Scrapena; the other," Jerry paused impressively, "was our precious hob-goblin, Miss Cairns."

CHAPTER III.

GATHERING CLOUDS.

"REALLY!" came in surprised exclamation from Vera.

"Hmm! What a congenial pair!" was Helen Trent's placid reception of the information.

"Like walks with like." Leila's tones vibrated with satirical truth. "Knaves fall out, but to fall in again."

"I know it," agreed Jerry. "One would naturally suppose that Miss Cairns would have no use for Row-ena after the net she led her into. Not a bit of it."

"It must have been a shock, Jeremiah, to look up suddenly and find yourself in such company." Helen could not repress the ghost of a chuckle.

"It was. They were lined up for battle. I saw that at a glance. Row-ena was half laughing; a trick of hers when she is all ready to make a grand disturbance. Leslie Cairns looked like a Japanese thundercloud. I never said a word; just sat very straight in my chair. I went on eating my ice as if I didn't know they were there. Like this."

Jerry gave an imitation of her manner and facial expression on the occasion she was describing.

"I thought they might give it up as a bad job and go away, but they stayed. Then Row-ena started in with a regular tirade about Marjorie and all of us. I can't repeat what she said word for word. Anyway, she called us all liars. I don't remember what I said, but it must have been effective. I certainly handed Row-ena my candid opinion of herself. She saw she was getting the worst of the argument and declared she wouldn't stay and be so insulted. She started out of the pavilion, calling Miss Cairns to come along. The fair Leslie wouldn't budge. She told Row-ena to go on, that she had something to say to me. That was the first remark she had made. Then she asked me in her slow, drawling way if I would listen to something she had to say to me. I said I would not. I had heard too much as it was. I got up and beat it and left her standing there. I was so sore I forgot to pay for my ice. I had to send Hal back with the money. As I started away from the pavilion, I saw Row-ena getting into a dizzy-looking black and white roadster. I think the car belonged to Miss Cairns. It looked like her. I suppose she and dear

Row-ena had been out for a ride and simply happened to run across me in the pavilion.

"Now comes the most interesting part of the story." Jerry glanced from one to another of her attentive little audience. "Three days afterward the postman left me a letter. The address was typed, so was the letter. When I opened it, I soon knew the writer. Here it is." Jerry produced a letter from a white kid bag she was carrying. "The distinguished writer of this letter is Leslie Cairns. I brought it along to read to you because what she has to say includes all of us. It's what I would call an open declaration of war. Listen to this:

" 'MISS MACY:

" 'Since you refused to listen to me the other day, I must resort to pen and ink to make you understand that when I have anything to say to a person I propose to say it. It isn't a case of what you want. It is a case of what I want. To begin with, I knew all about you and your pals before ever you came to Hamilton. My friend, Miss Farnham, heard that you were to enter Hamilton and warned me against all of you. I had you looked up, as I have powerful ways and means of doing this.

" 'As your friend, Miss Dean, the lying little hypocrite, had made my friend, Miss Farnham, so much trouble at high school, I decided to even her score for her. At first I did not intend to allow you to enter Hamilton at all. When I say "you" I include those dear chums of yours. My father could easily have arranged to keep you out of Hamilton. Then I concluded it would be better to let you come here and make things lively for you.

" 'I proposed that call on you ninnies on your first evening at college. We arranged matters so as to fuss you self-satisfied freshies a little and keep you from your dinner. We didn't care anything about meeting you, but we thought we might as well look you over. Miss Weyman gave it out that she would meet your party with her car on purpose to keep other students away. We wanted you to be a little bit lonesome. When you said in your room, that you saw Miss Weyman's car at the station, we thought perhaps you might have seen through the joke. But you were *so* thick. You didn't.

" 'Miss Weyman had no intention of wasting good gasoline on you. She loaded her car with girls on purpose. There was no room to spare. She stopped it above the station yard and stayed there until after the train had come in. After a while she drove into the yard and out again. Not one of us set foot on the platform. It was a clever bluff and served you precisely right.

" 'I haven't either the patience or the will to tell you all the clever stunts we put over on you simpletons last year. Believe me, when I say, it isn't a circumstance compared to what we intend to do this year. You came back at us in March in a way we will not forget or overlook. You think you are pretty strongly intrenched because you and your crowd are quite pally with certain upper class students who pose as wonders of smartness. Well, don't build too much on your popularity. Popularity sometimes has a habit of vanishing over night.

" 'It seems too bad to be wasting time and paper on you, but I am square enough to let you have the truth straight from the shoulder. You girls have made us trouble from the start, and I predict that it will not be long before Hamilton will be too small to hold your crowd and mine. Your crowd will be the one to go; not the Sans. I am not afraid to tell you this, because there is nothing in this letter that you can get me on.

" 'Leslie Cairns.' "

"That is so like Leslie Cairns." Leila's blue eyes flashed their profound contempt. "She loves to boast of her own ill-doing. She thinks it gives her a standing among her friends. She poses as being afraid of nothing and no one.

"That is truly an outrageous letter!" Vera's voice rang with shocked indignation. "I wonder at her boldness in writing it."

"Ah, but consider! It is a typed letter. Would you mind letting me look at the signature, Jerry?" Helen requested.

"With pleasure." Jerry willingly surrendered the typed letter to Helen.

The latter studied the signature shrewdly. "I don't think this is Leslie Cairns signature," she said, shaking her head. "That is about the way I thought it would be."

"Humph!" Leila had evidently caught Helen's meaning. The others looked a trifle mystified.

"But Leila just now said the letter sounded like Leslie Cairns!" Jerry exclaimed. "She wrote it. I am sure of that. Her name is signed to it. Why then——" Jerry stopped. "Oh, yes," she went on, in sudden enlightenment. "I begin to understand."

"Of course you do," returned Helen. "In the first place," she explained to her puzzled listeners, "this letter has neither date nor place of writing. It is typed and signed 'Leslie Cairns,' but I am almost positive she did not sign it. She has either disguised her hand or another person has signed her name to it at her request, you may be sure. Object—if Jerry decided to make her any trouble at Hamilton over the letter, she would say she had nothing whatever to do with the writing of it."

"It would take a whole lot of nerve to do that. After what happened last year, she could hardly hope to be believed." This was Muriel's view of the matter.

"Still, if the letter were typed and not signed by her, there would be no proof that she wrote it unless someone had seen her write it." Helen argued. "We are positive she wrote it, because the contents of the letter tally with the Sans' attitude and actions toward Marjorie and you Sandfordites. Yet, what would hinder her from saying that some friend of yours, to whom you had told your troubles, or, that even one of you five girls wrote that letter, simply for spite? I do not say that she would do so. I only say she might. She is capable of it."

"I agree with you, Helen. Leslie Cairns would stand before President Matthews and declare up and down that she never dreamed of writing such a letter, if it pleased her to do it." Leila spoke with conviction. "She took chances, of course, of being called to account for the statements she made in the letter. Undoubtedly, she had her whole course of action planned out before ever she wrote it. While she couldn't be sure you wouldn't make a fuss about it, because of the way Ronny brought the Sans to book last March, she could plan the best way to brazen it out if she got into difficulties over it.

"Just imagine! She had a grudge against the Lookouts before ever she met them. Leila and I were always suspicious of the way Natalie Weyman acted about meeting you at the station. We could not fathom the object of such a performance. We both thought there was more to it than appeared on the surface." Vera nodded wisely.

"And all on account of the maliciousness of Rowena Farnham. Why, none of us had seen her for over two years! We supposed she belonged to our departed high school days." Muriel's tones betrayed decided umbrage.

"You can make up your minds that I don't intend ever to serve on any reform committees—object, the betterment of the heathen; the Sans, I mean." Jerry made this announcement with a shade of belligerence. Unconsciously she turned her eyes toward Marjorie.

Marjorie laughed. "I know what you are thinking, Jeremiah," she said, with quiet amazement. "Don't worry. I shall not suggest a reform movement here for the Sans' moral benefit."

"Glad of it. Imagine me laboring patiently with that benighted heathen, Leslie Cairns, to help her to see herself as others see her," grumbled Jerry.

"How much the Sans would enjoy being called the heathen," interposed Katherine Langly.

"It's appropriate. When people behave like savages, they class themselves as such. It is a pity that we should be obliged to consider fellow students as enemies!" Jerry continued with vehemence. "Why should petty spite be carried to the point where it is a menace to the whole college? An institution for the higher education of young girls in particular should be free of such ignobility."

"Fights and fusses are not conducive to the cultivation of a scholarly mind," Helen Trent agreed with mock solemnity.

"They are not," returned Leila, with a strong Celtic inflection of which she, in her earnestness, was entirely unconscious.

Naturally it evoked laughter. Leila's occasional slight lapses into a brogue were invariably amusing to her chums.

"Laugh at my brogue if you wish, I will not break your bones," she said good-humoredly, making use of an ancient Irish expression. "I am most Celtic when serious. Ah, well! Perhaps it is petty in us even to be discussing the Sans, since we can say nothing good of them."

"That is their fault; not ours," Lucy Warner said incisively.

"The fault, dear Brutus, lies not in their stars, but in themselves, that they are underlings," Vera aptly applied with a change of pronouns.

"Quite right, my child." They began it. Not one of us, before the Lookouts came here to Hamilton, raised a voice against the Sans. We know the Lookouts did not. This letter Leslie Cairns wrote to Jerry means war to the knife, all this year. Unless, by good fortune, Miss Remson has won her point and they are not to come back to the Hall. With them out of Wayland Hall we might hope for peace. Put them in other campus houses, they would soon lose track of you girls and turn their bad attentions to or on someone else. Miss Remson has a strong case against them on account of the way they treated Marjorie." Such was Helen's opinion.

Marjorie flushed at mention of the Sans' bad treatment of herself. She glanced at Ronny, who returned the glance with an enigmatical smile. Leila was staring at Marjorie, her face also a study.

"Girls," Marjorie began, in her clear resonant enunciation, "I shall have to tell you something that only Ronny and Leila know. I told Leila only this afternoon. I asked Miss Remson not to mention the Sans' treatment of me in her complaint to the president. I had a long talk with her last June before college closed. I asked Ronny if she cared if I did so, because she had gone to the trouble of getting Miss Archer here and spared no pains to help me. All of you helped me, too, but Ronny and Miss Remson did the hardest part. Ronny said I must do whatever my conscience dictated. I felt that I did not wish to have anything to do with

their leaving the Hall. If Miss Remson wins or
has won her point against them, that's different.
Last March, before we held the meeting in the living room, it seemed as if I could not endure being
under the same roof with them. That feeling
passed away. They were so utterly defeated. Miss
Remson says she has enough insubordinate and
really lawless acts on their part against them to
warrant their being transferred to another campus
house. She said it had been done occasionally in
past years with beneficial results."

"That means the Sans will be at the Hall again
this year." Resentment burned briefly in Helen's
eyes. Slow to anger, she was slower to forgive.

"We don't know that yet," resumed Ronny.
"All this happened last June. Miss Remson made
her complaint then, I believe. She intended to, at
any rate. Naturally, we could not ask her about the
result, and she said nothing more about it before
we went home. I think she will mention it to Marjorie and me. If she does we will ask if we may
tell you girls who were interested in the affair of
last March."

"We'll know anyway, if the Sans appear bag
and baggage," put in practical Lucy.

"Yes; but I mean Miss Remson will tell us the
details," returned Ronny.

"Wherever the Sans live on the campus, our best

way is to go on about our own affairs regardless
of them. I hate to think of Hamilton College as
a battle ground. I will fight for my rights, if I
must, but I will ignore a worthless enemy as long
as I can. We must make our plans for a happier
Hamilton, which does not include the Sans. We
must create a spirit of unity here that will discount
cliques." Marjorie argued with deep earnestness.
"If we fight, shoulder to shoulder, for the best, in
time we shall attain it. It's our influence that will
count. It may not be felt at once; gradually it
will be. We need not expect the Sans will change
their views. We must put them in the background
by being true and kindly and honorable. Then
their false standards will count for nothing."

CHAPTER IV.

AN INVITATION TO AN "OFFICE PARTY."

I'M very, very sleepy, Jeremiah, but I shall try
to keep awake for the chimes. It would be unkind
not to greet my second friend tonight." Marjorie
made these whimsical statements between yawns.

"Wait for 'em, then, if you can," returned Jerry.
"The minute my head touches the pillow I shall be
dead to the world. You'll never keep awake. You
are yawning now."

"I shall," firmly avowed Marjorie. Tired out by
the long railway journey, her eyes would close.
Nevertheless she slipped into a silk negligee and
curled up on the floor beside a window, to wait for
the welcoming voice of her loved friend. The
light in the room extinguished, the white moonlight
touched her sweet face, lending it a new and wist-
ful beauty. From her post at the window she could
see Hamilton Hall, a magnificent gray pile in the
moonbeams. The campus stretched away on all
sides of it like an enchanted emerald carpet full of
lights and shadows.

Marjorie momentarily forgot her desire for sleep, as she looked on the silent loveliness which night had enhanced. It filled her with all sorts of vague inspirations which she could sense but not analyze. She could only understand herself as being earnestly desirous of showing greater loyalty to her 'Alma Mater than ever before.

Then upon her inspirited musings fell the voice of her old, familiar friend, clear and silvery as ever. She sat very still, almost breathlessly, listening to the clarion, welcoming prelude. Followed the measured stroke of eleven. "I am so happy to hear you again, dear friend. Good night." Marjorie rose, and, with a last, sleepy, but loving, glance at the fairylike outdoors trotted to her couch bed. She had scarcely found its grateful comfort before she was fast asleep.

She awoke the next morning with the sunshine pouring in upon her to find Jerry, kimono-clad, standing meditatively beside her couch.

"Why—um—what—where——" she mumbled. "Oh, goodness, Jerry! have I overslept? What time is it? That wall clock stopped last night just after we came in, and I forgot to wind it and set it again." She sat up hastily.

"Be calm," replied Jerry, with a reassuring grin. "It is only five minutes to seven. I was wondering whether I could let you sleep fifteen minutes more.

I'd decided to call you when you woke of your own accord."

"I'd rather be up." Marjorie arose with her customary energy and reached for her negligee. "I have a lot to do today. Our trunks will be here by noon, I hope. I want to unpack and be all straightened out before the five o'clock train. Leila and Vera are anxious for us to go with them to meet it. We ought to meet it at any rate. We are both on the sophomore committee for welcoming freshies."

Marjorie made this reminder with open satisfaction. During Commencement week, the previous June, the sophomore class elect had gathered for a special meeting. Its object had been to discuss ways and means of helping entering freshmen at the re-opening of college in the fall. Marjorie and Jerry had been appointed to it as Wayland Hall representatives, together with two students from Acasia House and three from Silverton Hall.

"I imagine we are the only ones on that committee who have come back to Hamilton," Marjorie continued. "Oh, no; Ethel Laird is on it. Let me see. Grace Dearborn was the other Acasia House girl appointed. Blanche Scott, Elaine Hunter and Miss Peyton were the three from Silverton Hall. Ronny said none of them had returned."

"I am almost sorry I did not make arrangements

to have a car here this year." Jerry looked slightly regretful. "It would come in handy now. Still, I believe it is more democratic to do without one. Besides, I ought to walk rather than ride. It keeps my weight down. There is Ronny. She could have a dozen cars here if she wanted them. She won't have one. She is a real democrat, isn't she?"

Marjorie nodded. "She is the most unassuming very rich girl I have ever known. I think if the Sans really knew her circumstances they would try to take her up, even after what happened last spring."

"They would give it up as too hard a job about five minutes after Ronny found out what they were trying to do," predicted Jerry. "I have an idea that the Sans think we don't amount to much financially. My father is worth a whole lot of money, yet it's not generally known in Sanford. He never tried to keep it a secret, but you see we have never gone in for anything but the quiet family life. So people don't think much about us, except that we are old Sanford residents."

"That is a fine way to live," thoughtfully approved Marjorie. "Well, I couldn't afford to have a car here if I wanted one ever so much. The majority of the girls at Hamilton are probably from families in about the same circumstances as the Deans. Leila said yesterday that about a third of the girls here last year had their own automobiles. She said she would have been terribly lonely during her freshman year if she had not had her car. She didn't send for it for quite awhile after she entered college. Vera sent for hers, too, and hardly drove it. Most of the freshmen they were friendly with had their own cars, so they seldom needed to drive both cars at the same time."

As she talked, Marjorie had been leisurely but steadily gathering up her toilet accessories preparatory to making her morning ablutions. Jerry, who stood idly watching her chum, suddenly realized that time was on the wing.

"Good gracious!" she exclaimed. "Here I stand like a dummy when I ought to be hiking for the lavatory myself. We'll both be late for breakfast, in spite of my early rising, if we stop to talk any longer. After breakfast we had better 'phone the baggage master about our trunks. Otherwise they may forget all about us and not deliver them before tomorrow. I haven't the trusting faith in baggage masters that I might have."

In the lavatory they encountered Muriel and Ronny. Lucy had already preceded them and gone to pay Katherine a morning call. Presently the Five Travelers and Katherine trooped down the wide stairway to breakfast, their bright, youthful faces and clear, laughing tones lending new life to staid Wayland Hall. At the foot of the stairway, they met Miss Remson and hailed her with a concerted "Good morning."

Her small, shred eyes softened, as she received the gay salute with a smile and returned it. Her liking for this particular sextette of students was very sincere.

"Girls," she began abruptly, her smile fading, to be replaced by an expression of sternness, "Will you come into my office after breakfast? I have something to show you and also something to tell you." Her lips tightened to grimness as she made this announcement. "That's all." With a little nod she passed them and hurried on up the staircase.

As she had been busily engaged with the affairs of the Hall on their arrival of the preceding afternoon, they had had opportunity only to greet her and be assigned to their old rooms and places at table.

Entering the dining room, Vera and Leila called "Good morning" from the next table to their own.

"Be with you in a minute," Leila informed them. "I've something to report, Lieutenant." This directly to Marjorie. During the Easter visit she and Vera had made Marjorie, she had taken delightedly to the army idea as carried out by the Deans.

Afterward she frequently addressed Marjorie as "Lieutenant."

"I know what it is," promptly returned Jerry. "So have we. We just saw Miss Remson. Is that what you are driving at?"

"It is. Now what shall I do to you for snapping my news from my mouth?" Leila asked severely.

"Maybe I don't know as much as you do, so you needn't feel grieved," conciliated Jerry. "Come over here and we will compare notes. I may know something you don't know. You may know something I don't know. Think what a wonderful information session we shall have."

Hurriedly finishing her coffee, Leila rose and joined the Lookouts. "I won't sit down," she declined, as Ronny motioned her to draw up a nearby chair. "Miss Remson asked Vera and I to stop at her office after breakfast."

"She asked us, too. There, I took Jerry's news away from her. That pays up for what she did to you." Muriel glanced teasingly at Jerry.

"Oh, go as far as you like." Jerry waved an elaborately careless hand. "Like the race in Alice in Wonderland: 'All won.' Perhaps one of you wise women of Hamilton can tell us if anyone else is invited to Busy Buzzy's office party."

"Silence was the answer," put in Marjorie mischievously, as no one essayed a reply to Jerry's satirical question.

"Helen ought to be," Jerry said stoutly. "She was with us to the letter last spring. I guess she'll be there. Miss Remson is fond of her."

One and all the eight girls were experiencing inward satisfaction at the summons to Miss Remson's office. Confident that it had to do with the re-admittance or denial of the Sans to Wayland Hall, they were glad that the odd little manager had chosen to give them her confidence.

"I'm going over to the garage to see if the new tire is on my car. It blew out yesterday while I was driving it to cover after I left you girls. I'll be back by the time you girls have finished breakfast. Going with me, Midget?" Leila turned to Vera.

"No, Ireland," she declined, with the little rippling smile which was one of her chief charms. "I am still hungry. I want another cup of coffee and a nice fat cinnamon bun. By the time I put them away you will be back."

As Leila went out, Helen Trent appeared, a slightly sleepy look in her blue eyes. Her arrival was greeted with acclamation. Aside from Vera and Leila, the long pleasant dining room was empty of students when the Lookouts and Katherine had entered it. In consequence, they were more free to laugh and talk. The presence of the Sans in the

room during meals quenched the spirit of comrad-
arie that was so marked at Silverton Hall.

"Have you seen Miss Remson?" was hurled at
Helen in chorus. She dimpled engagingly and
nodded her head.

"I saw her last night after I left you girls. I
had to have a new bulb for one of my lights."

"Glad of it." Jerry beamed at Helen. She had
not wished her junior friend left out of Miss Remson's confidence. "If she had not told you, I was
going to ask her if you might be in on it," she
assured.

"Faithful old Jeremiah." Helen reached over
from where she had paused beside the Lookouts'
table and patted Jerry on the shoulder.

"One might think you were addressing a valued
family watch dog," remarked Lucy Warner. Hel-
en's dimples deepened. "You don't say much,
Luciferous, but what you say is *amazin'*. I hadn't
the slightest intention of ranking my respected
pardner, Jeremiah, as an animal friend. With this
apologetic explanation, I shall insist that you drop
all such thoughts."

"Oh, I did not say I thought so," calmly cor-
rected Lucy. "I merely said, 'One might think.'
Lucy's features were purposely austere. Her greenish eyes were dancing. Long since her chums had

discovered that her sense of humor was as keen as her sense of criticism.

Leila presently returned to find the breakfasters feasting on hot, old-fashioned cinnamon buns. These buns were a specialty at Wayland Hall, and, with coffee, were a tempting meal in themselves. Another ten minutes, and they left the dining room en masse, bound for the little manager's office, there to learn what they might or might not expect from the Sans during the coming college year.

CHAPTER V.

LETTER NUMBER TWO.

"COME in!" called a brisk, familiar voice, as Ronny knocked lightly on the almost closed door. Filing decorously into the rather small office, the nine girls grouped themselves about the manager's chair.

"Take seats, friends," she invited. "Four of you can use the settee. There are chairs enough for the others. Will you see that the door is tightly closed, Helen. This matter is strictly confidential. It's rather early for eavesdroppers," she added, with biting sarcasm.

"The door is closed, Miss Remson." Having complied with the manager's request, Helen seated herself beside Jerry on a wide walnut bench which took up almost a side of the room.

"Thank you. You know, my dear young friends," Miss Remson began, with out further preliminary, "that, last March, after Miss Dean's trouble with the Sans Soucians, I expressed myself as being heartily sick of their lawless behavior. I stated then that I should take up the matter with President Matthews. I believed he would respect my point of view. I had made up my mind that I did not wish them to return to the Hall this year. Wayland Hall is the oldest and finest house on the campus. Naturally, it is hard to obtain board here. I have been here longer than any other manager of any other Hamilton campus house. I have rarely made complaint against a student. Miss Dean was anxious that I should not put her case before President Matthews. I could only respect her wishes, as the matter was strictly personal. There were many other reasons why the Sans Soucians, as they call themselves, were undesirable boarders."

Miss Remson ceased speaking momentarily, as she separted a letter from two or three others on her desk.

"These girls, of whom I disapproved, made the usual application to retain their rooms. I made a list of the undesirables and went over to the president's house to have a confidential talk with him. I have known him and his family for years. Unfortunately, he was not at home. He had been invited to make an address at the Commencement of Newbold, a western college for women, and would be away for a week. As his return would be so near Commencement here, I decided to write him and ask for an early appointment. I wrote to him as soon as he returned. He answered my note personally and made an appointment with me.

"I laid my complaint before him," she continued, "and he was indignant at the way I had been treated. He asked me to leave with him the names of the young women against whom I had made complaint. He promised they should be reprimanded by him and notified to make other arrangements for this college year. Further, they would also be warned that any new complaints against them from another manager would mean a second summons to his office, with a more severe penalty attached.

"I waited, expecting a storm when these girls received their notification and learned what I had done. I had not given them an answer regarding their rooms for next year, as I was waiting for Doctor Matthews to act. Judge my surprise when, five days after I had talked with the doctor, I received a cool note, dictated to his secretary, stating that he was inclosing a typed copy of a letter which he had received. He went on to say that, as there seemed to be as much complaint against me, by the young women of whom I had complained, he would suggest that we get together and try to adjust the matter at the Hall. He believed that the course I had requested him to pursue would result in such useless ill-feeling that he preferred not to adopt it.

He had no doubt that an internal friction, such as appeared to exist at Wayland Hall, could be easily adjusted by me, if I adopted the proper methods. He wished the subject closed."

"Why, that isn't a bit like Doctor Matthews!" exclaimed Helen. "He has the reputation of being a stickler for justice."

"My dear, I know it," replied Miss Remson, in a hurt voice. "I felt utterly crushed after I had read his note. There was nothing more to be done unless I resigned. I did not wish to do so. I have every right to retain my position here. It is my living and I do a great deal for my sister's two sons, whom I am helping put through college. The copy of the letter, inclosed with the president's note, was written by Miss Myers. I shall read it to you verbatim."

Unfolding the copied letter which she held in her hand, she hastily read the formal heading then went on more slowly:

"DEAR DOCTOR MATTHEWS:

"It has been intimated us that we are not to be granted the privilege of remaining at Wayland Hall during our junior year. We understand the reason for this injustice and wish you to understand it also. Miss Remson, the manager of the Hall, has taken sides with a certain few students in the

house who have a fancied grudge against a number
of young women whose interests I am now repre-
senting. Miss Remson has allowed these students
to place us in the most humiliating of positions; has
even aided and abetted them in putting us in a false
light. She has also reprimanded us frequently for
offenses of which we are not guilty. We are willing to overlook all this and try even more earnestly
in future to please Miss Remson. This, in spite of
the harsh way in which we have been treated by all
concerned. We are not willing to leave the Hall.
We came here to live as freshmen and we object
to being thrust from it after two years' residence in
it. We have been given to understand that complaint against us is to be lodged with you by Miss
Remson. Will you not take up the matter summarily with her and see that we obtain justice?

"Yours sincerely,

"JOAN MYERS."

A united gasp arose as Miss Remson finished the
reading of Joan Myers' letter and laid it on the
desk.

"Can you beat that?" inquired Jerry, in such
deep disgust everyone laughed. "Of all the cast-
iron, nickle-plated nerve, commend me to the Sans."

"Outrageous!" Leila's black brows were drawn
in a deep scowl. "And they are clever, too," she

nodded with conviction. "That letter is the kind a man of Doctor Matthews' standing detests. It gives the whole affair the air of a school-girl quarrel. Very hard on your dignity, Miss Remson," she glanced sympathetically at the little manager.

"Not only that. I am practically cut off from my old friendly standing with the president." Miss Remson's usually quick tones faltered slightly. "I would not appeal to him for justice again if these lawless girls brought the Hall down about my ears. You can understand my position."

She appealed to her youthful hearers in general. "It was my belief that you should be told this by me, as I had assured you last spring that I would not have these trouble-making, untruthful students at the Hall this year, if I could help it. They are coming back wholly against my will. We were into Commencement week last June when this occurred, so I said nothing to any of you. It would have been an annoyance to you during the summer every time you happened to recall it."

"Who told the Sans that you weren't going to allow them to come back to the Hall?" was Marjorie's pertinent question. "I can answer for every one of us in saying that we never repeated a word outside of our own intimate circle."

"That is a question I have pondered more than once during the summer," Miss Remson responded with alacrity. "I did not suspect one of you for an instant. I do not see how anyone could have overheard the remarks I made on the subject, as I made them in this office with the door always closed. President Matthews is, of course, above suspicion. His secretary would not dare repeat his official business, even to an intimate friend. I mailed my letter to the president. It went through the postoffice. This precludes the possibility of it having been tampered with."

"Perhaps the Sans guessed that you would refuse them admittance to the Hall this year because you called the meeting in the living room," was Muriel's plausible surmise. "You had had a good deal of trouble with them and they knew they were in the wrong; that you disapproved of them. They may have scented disaster and taken the bull by the horns. They calculated, perhaps, that you might appeal to President Matthews and thought they would secure themselves by reporting us and accusing you of favoritism."

"That would be typical of the Sans," agreed Leila energetically. "Not so much Leslie Cairns. She bribes and bullies her way to whatever she wants. Joan Myers wrote the letter. She is considered very clever among her crowd. She may have made the plan. Dulcie Vale is too stupid and Nat Weyman is wrapped up in herself."

"A clever letter, contemptible though it is," pronounced Veronica. The writer has put a certain amount of force in it which passes for sincerity."

"It reads as though she had been informed that Miss Remson was going to turn the Sans down and was honestly sore over it." Jerry added her speculation to Ronny's.

"It is too bad!" exclaimed Helen Trent, indignantly. "I mean for you, Miss Remson. You can soon find out for yourself whether they simply guessed you were down on them or really had information. When the Sans come back to the Hall, if they are snippy and insolent from the start, that will mean, I think, that they had warning of it. If they are rather subdued and fairly civil, for them, then they only made a daring bluff and are not sure, up to date, whether their suspicion was correct."

"Great head!" laughingly complimented Jerry. "There is nothing the mater with Helen's reasoning powers."

Miss Remson nodded slowly as she considered Helen's words. "That is very likely the way it will be," she said. "The matter will have to remain closed, because President Matthews wishes it to be so. I shall not adopt his suggestion of a personal talk with these girls." A glint of belligerence appeared in her eyes. "I have been here at the Hall many years and seen many young women come and go. I am not a bad judge of girl character and motive. It will not take me long to fathom these girls' deceit in this affair, if the letter Miss Myers wrote was based on supposition. If, in some unprecedented manner, they really received information, then they must have learned the outcome of the affair from the same source. All I can do is to remain mute on the subject. They will, undoubtedly, ridicule me behind my back. If they attempt to belittle me to my face, I shall resign my position here." The humiliated little manager's lips compressed into a tight line.

"I think the whole business is shameful; simply shameful!" burst forth Vera, her blue eyes flashing. "Imagine President Matthews taking such an extremely unjust stand!"

"It is too bad you cannot go to him and have the matter out with him. No; I understand that you wouldn't, under the circumstances," Jerry added quickly, as Miss Remson made a hasty gesture of dissent. I wouldn't either, if I were you."

"I believe there is more to this than appears on the surface," Marjorie gave steady opinion. "We hardly know President Matthews, as we were merely freshies last year. Still he seems to be such a fine man. A man in his position ought to be above anything even touching on injustice."

"There you are! 'Seems to be,' and 'ought to

be,' " repeated Leila cynically. "May I ask you, Miss Remson, do you know the signature to the president's letter to you to be by his own hand? I would not hesitate to set a trumped-up letter down to the Sans' mischief-making bureau."

"Yes; it is President Matthews' signature; unmistakably his," answered Miss Remson. "I am satisfied Doctor Matthews wrote the letter. It is written much as he would write if he were thoroughly annoyed. Neither Miss Myers nor her friends could write it. You spoke of there being more to this than appears on the surface, Miss Dean. Pardon me for disagreeing. I hardly think so."

Marjorie never forgot the hurt look that crept into the manager's usually cheerful face as she bravely disagreed. It was as though she had caught a glimpse of the plucky little woman's grieving soul. She realized that Miss Remson had found it hard to give even them her confidence. She guessed also that the manager would be grateful if left to herself.

"I know what it means to feel dreadfully hurt over something untrue that has been said of one, Miss Remson," she consoled in her sincere, gracious fashion. "That's the way it was with me last March. Thanks to my friends, the clouds blew away and the sun came out again. We are your true friends, and we would like to do as much for you as we know you have done for me, and would do for any of us who needed your support. We solemnly promise," she went on, turning to her chums for corroboration, "to regard your confidence as binding. Not one of us will forget the hurt that has been dealt you. We shall do our best to make it easier for you at the Hall by keeping clear of the Sans."

"Miss Remson, I feel positive that Doctor Matthews will realize, later, what a serious mistake he has made. Sometimes the very finest men make just such blunders because they are irritated by something else entirely." Katherine spoke with deep conviction. "I acted as secretary one summer to a naturalist who was of that type."

"There is one thing I intend to do." Lucy Warner spoke for the first time since entering the office. She had listened with the gravity and attention of a judge to all that had been said. "I shall make it a point to see what President Matthews' secretary looks like. A secretary has a good deal of opportunity to make trouble, if she chooses to make it. She knows so much of her employer's private affairs. I've been a secretary long enough to tell you that. She might have quietly told the Sans of Miss Remson's letter to the president, asking for an interview."

"But, my dear child, I did not mention the object

of my interview in my note to President Matthews," declared the manager. "The secretary would have nothing to tell these girls of any moment. She would naturally attach no importance to such a letter."

"That is true." Lucy looked abashed for an instant. Her old shyness seemed about to settle down on her. She cast it off and sat up very straight, her green eyes gleaming with her initial purpose. "I believe I will look her up, at any rate. She might be a friend of the Sans."

"Hardly," differed Muriel. "The Sans don't make a friend of a girl under the million mark, Lucy."

"Unless it happens to suit their purpose," flatly contradicted Lucy, with no intent to be rude. "They are the very persons who would pretend friendship with a poor girl if they thought she would be useful to them. There are girls who would feel highly flattered to be taken up by them. I can't pass opinion upon this secretary until I have seen her. Perhaps not until I have seen her a number of times."

"Luciferous Warniferous, the world's great private investigator." Despite the seriousness of the occasion, Muriel could not refrain from venturing this pleasantry.

"You needn't make fun of me." Lucy laughed

with the others. "It won't do any harm, at least, to view her from afar."

"I thank you all for your interest in me and for your promise." Miss Remson surveyed the group of youthful sympathizers through a slight mist. "Don't keep this in mind, girls," she counseled. "It is better forgotten. I shall try to get along with this disagreeable flock of students with the least possible friction. If they take advantage of this victory, which they have gained unfairly, and attempt to override my authority at the Hall, I shall resign at once."

CHAPTER VI.

THE GENUS "FRESHMAN."

LEAVING the manager's office, soon afterward, the nine girls would have liked nothing better than to repair to one of their rooms and discuss the subject of Miss Remson's grievances at length. All had the liveliest sympathy for the kindly official and longed to do something to prove it. Unfortunately, nearly all of them had work to do or engagements to keep. The Sanford contingent had their trunks to unpack as soon as they should arrive. They hoped that would be very soon. Katherine had made an engagement with Lillian Wenderblatt to go for a long walk. Leila and Vera were going to drive to the town of Hamilton to buy the wherewithal for a spread to be given that evening in honor of Nella and Selma, who were expected on the five o'clock train. Helen being the only one with time on her hands, Leila advised her to join them on their quest for the most toothsome "eats."

Contrary to Jerry's wet-blanket and extravagant

prediction that the trunks would probably be delivered "around midnight," they arrived shortly before eleven o'clock, and an industrious season of unpacking set in. Determined to finish arranging their effects before four o'clock, they labored at the task with commendable energy and speed, stopping only for luncheon, which was eaten in some haste.

"We certainly have hustled," Jerry congratulated, as she lifted the last remaining articles from the bottom of one of her two trunks and found place for them in her chiffonier. "Im glad the job is done. We shall have lots of time to take it easy. Here it is, only Wednesday. College doesn't open officially until next Tuesday. We have nearly a week to ourselves."

"We'll begin today to look after the freshies," planned Marjorie. "Then we must meet one train a day, if not two, until we are not needed any longer. I shall stick rigidly to that work on account of the welcome we were cheated of last September."

"What are you going to wear to the train this afternoon?" Jerry inquired, critically inspecting two or three frocks she had laid out on her couch bed. She was uncertain which one to wear.

"That one." Marjorie nodded toward a chair over which hung a one-piece frock of fine white linen. "I think white looks nicest when one is going to the station. I love to wear my white dresses as late in the fall as I can."

"Then I'll wear white, too." Jerry immediately selected a pretty lingerie gown and sighed relief to have that matter off her mind. "I am going the rounds and tell the gang to wear white, by order of the Board of Suitable Suits for Auspicious Occasions. Back in a minute."

Glancing at the clock, which showed ten minutes past four, Marjorie hurriedly slipped out of the pink gingham dress she had been wearing and took the white linen frock from the chair. She had been making leisurely preparations for the trip to the station while Jerry finished unpacking.

"I can plainly see my finish." Jerry presently entered the room with a bounce, seized a towel from the washstand and bounced out again. She returned as breezily within a few minutes and continued her toilet at the same rate of speed. Leila had said: "Not one minute later than four-thirty," and Jerry did not propose to be left behind.

"Are the rest of the crowd going to wear white?" Marjorie asked, giving her wealth of curly hair a final touch before the mirror.

"Yes; but it's just a happen-so. Most of them were dressed for the auspicious occasion when I arrived on the scene. Their suits were suitable, so I beat it back here in a hurry. Please tie my sash for me, Marjorie, while I labor some more with my aggravating hair. I swear I will have it cropped like Robin Page's."

"She'll have hers done up when she comes back," commented Marjorie, deftly complying with Jerry's request. "It was almost long enough to do up last June and she was proud of it."

"I hope Robin comes in on the five o'clock train. I'd like to see her. Next to Helen, I like her best of the Hamiltonites."

The entrance of Ronny, also in white linen, with the information that Muriel and Lucy had gone on down stairs to the veranda, cut short Jerry's remarks. The three girls reached the veranda at precisely four-thirty, to find Leila's and Vera's cars on the drive in readiness to start.

Through the glory of late afternoon sunlight the two cars, each with its winsome freight of white-gowned girls, sped down the smooth pike past beautiful Hamilton Estates and on toward the station. Happy in the fact that she was now so perfectly at home at Hamilton, Marjorie smiled as she compared last year with the present. Yes; it was good to be a sophomore. Her new estate stretched invitingly before her. It was all so very different from the previous September. The splendor of the sunlit sky and the warm fragrance of the light breeze seemed indicative of pleasant days to come.

Because she had missed a welcome on her arrival at Hamilton, she was ready to welcome doubly some other freshman stranger within Hamilton's gates.

"Train 16, late, 40 minutes," was the dampening information which stared them in the face from the station bulletin board.

"Forty minutes! Who cares to eat ice cream? Back into the buzz wagons, all of you. I like the taste of ice cream in my mouth better than the feel of those station boards under my feet for a long stretch of forty minutes. We can go to the Ivy, that little white shop on Linden Avenue. It is only two blocks from the station. We shall have time and to spare."

Leila called the latter part of her remarks over her shoulder. Immediately she had read the notice she turned and started for the station yard. Her companions followed her with alacrity. They were no more in favor than she of a tedious wait on the platform for a belated train.

"One of us had better call time," wisely suggested Helen, as they flocked into the pretty white and green tea room. "Otherwise we are likely to overstay our limit. We must be out of here ten minutes before the train is due. You had better, Luciferous. You are infallible."

"Much obliged." A faint pink crept into Lucy's fair pale skin. Lucy was secretly proud of her own reliability. Turning her pretty gold wrist watch on her wrist so that she could see the face of it, she watched it with an eager eye from then on. The watch had been a gift to her from Ronny the previous Christmas, and was her most valued possession.

Fortune favored them with prompt service on the part of a waitress. They had only comfortably finished their ice cream, however, when Lucy announced that it was time to go. Returning to the station platform, they found only a sprinkling of students awaiting the coming train.

"What has become of Ethel Laird, I wonder?" asked Jerry. "I hope she hasn't forgotten she is on this welcoming committee. Suppose about twenty or thirty freshmen stepped off the five o'clock train. It would keep Marjorie and me busy chasing up and down this old board walk handing out welcomes."

"Now where do you suppose we would be during that time?" demanded Leila.

"Oh, you would be a help, undoubtedly," conceded Jerry, with a boyish grin. I forgot about you folks. I was merely thinking of us from our committee standpoint. We'll have to guess whether these arrivals are freshies or not. I don't know all the Hamilton students and where they belong. It will be about my speed to walk up to some timid-looking damsel and gallantly offer my assistance only to find out she is a proud and lofty senior."

"There are few faces at Hamilton which I don't know," Leila assured. "Behave well and stick to me and I'll promise you will not do anything foolish. I can pick a freshie from afar off."

"Miss Remson told me yesterday that she understood there were one hundred and ten freshmen applications this year," said Katherine. "We are to have three freshies at Wayland Hall."

"One hundred and ten democrats would help our cause along," remarked Lucy. "Only we need not expect any such miracle."

"With the start we now have, if even half of the freshmen were for college equality, it would be a hard blow to the Sans. I wish it might be like that." Vera clasped her bits of hands, an unconsciously pretty fashion of hers when she earnestly desired something to come to pass.

"The Sans will fight for every inch of the ground this year. See if they don't" Katherine Langly spoke with half bitter conviction. "Do you think for an instant that they will sit still and see democracy win? Leslie Cairns loves power. Joan Myers is determined to have her own way. Natalie Weymain is vain. Dulcie Vale is vindictive. Evangeline Heppler and Adelaide Forman are thoroughly disagreeable. Margaret Wayne is malicious and scandalously untruthful. There! That is my can-

'did opinion of those seven students. I have always longed to express it."

"I see you have found your tongue. I congratulate you." Leila beamed approval of such refreshing frankness on the part of quiet little Katherine.

"We had better enter a conspiracy to spend our spare time rushing freshies," proposed Helen. "When they are with us they will be out of mischief."

"First catch your hare," advised Muriel. "Maybe the freshies would not take kindly to the continuous round of pleasure we arranged for them. I don't believe there is any one infallible method of winning them over."

"Oh, I wasn't serious," Helen said, with her roguish, indolent smile. "While I don't object to helping the great cause along, I am not yearning to become a polite entertainer. I'd probably be a most impolite one before the end of a week, if I had to rush freshies as a steady task. I am afraid few of them would turn out to be as amiable, beautiful, jolly, delightful, agreeable and companionable as good old Jeremiah here."

"An awful waste of adjectives," was Jerry's terse reception of this extravagant tribute to herself. "Here comes the train." Despite her lack of sentiment, she flashed Helen a smile of comradeship.

The belated express thundered into the station

with a force which shook the platform. Instinct-
ively the scattered groups of persons on the platform drew back a trifle as the first three coaches
shot past. It was a long train and it did not take
more than a second glance down its length to note
that the last coach was quite different from the
others.

"Private car!" Leila's low exclamation held
more than surprise. It was sarcastically significant.
"Behold the Philistines are upon us," she continued in pretended consternation.

"We needn't mind a little thing like that," Jerry
assured with a genial smile. "They won't be met
and fussed over by us. I wonder where the mob is
who ought to be at the station to greet these celebrated geese?"

"They certainly chose a poor day for a triumphal
return." Muriel indulged in a soft chuckle at the
Sans' expense. She broke off in the middle of it
with a jubilant cry of, "Girls; there's Mortense just
getting off the train three coaches up the platform!"

"Hooray! Nella and Selma are with her!" This
from Leila, whose eyes had picked up dignified Hortense Barlow descending the car steps immediately
Muriel had cried out. Following her were the two
juniors of whom Leila and Vera were so fond.

The unwelcome Sans entirely forgotten, Leila,
Muriel and Vera headed an orderly rush up the

platform. All of the station party were anxious to give the three juniors a hearty reception. Marjorie and Ronny happened to be the last of the little procession. The former bore in mind her chief object in coming to the station and kept a sharp lookout for freshmen.

Just as they reached the edge of the group which had closed in about the three arrivals, Marjorie's searching eyes spied a small, flaxen-haired young woman with wide-opened blue eyes and a babyish expression, coming toward her. The latter was burdened with a heavy seal traveling case and a bag of golf sticks. She had evidently emerged from the coach behind the one from which Nella and her two companions had come. As she advanced, she gazed about her with a slightly perplexed air.

"Pardon me." Marjorie had stepped instantly to her side. "Are you a freshman? I am Marjorie Dean, of the sophomore class, and hope I can be of service to you. I am one of a sophomore committee to welcome arriving freshmen."

"Oh, thank you. Delighted, I'm sure, to know you, Miss Dean." The newcomer's conventionally courteous tone conveyed no particular enthusiasm. "Yes; I am a freshman. At least, I hope so. I have one exam. to try. I flunked in geometry at the prep school I attended last year. Had a tutor all summer. Guess I'll scrape through this time."

"I hope you will," Marjorie made sincere return. She half offered a hand to the other girl. The latter did not appear to see it. She clung tightly to her bag of golf sticks and traveling case. Far from paying undivided attention to Marjorie, her wide blue eyes roved over the platform, the light of curiosity strong within them.

"Hamilton must be a slow old college if it can't show more of a station mob than this," she remarked, almost disdainfully. "I mean it must be rather well—humdrum. I was at Welden Prep last year. It is a mighty lively school. It takes the Welden girls to properly mob the station. Oh, we were a gay crowd, I can tell you! Awfully select, you know, but really full of life."

"You will find Hamilton lively enough, I believe. It is early yet. A few of us are back earlier than usual. Not more than a fifth of the students have returned yet." Marjorie's tone was kindly. She made a patient effort to keep reserve out of it. Her first impression of the dissatisfied freshman was not pleasing.

"Oh, I see. I am glad there is hope." The girl gave a vacant little laugh. "I do so hate anything slow or poky or stupid. I had supposed Hamilton to be very smart and exclusive, or I wouldn't have chosen to come here."

"It is a very fine college. There is no better

faculty in the country, and the college itself is ideally located. You cannot help but love the campus. At which house are you to live?" Marjorie chose not to discuss Hamilton from the freshman's point of view.

"Alston Terrace. Is it an interesting house to live in? Where do you live? Are the garage accommodations good? I shall have my own car here; perhaps two. How far is it from the station to the campus?"

The stranger hurled these questions at Marjorie all in a breath. The latter's inclination toward secret vexation increased rather than diminished. Her fresman find was showing somewhat Sans-like tendencies.

"All the campus houses are interesting. I live at Wayland Hall. There are several garages in the vicinity of the college. It is about two miles from the station to Hamilton. If you will come with me, I will introduce you to some of my friends. A number of us came to the station together; some of us to meet friends expected on this train. Miss Macy, my room-mate, and myself are on the committee. Let me help you with your luggage."

Marjorie deftly possessed herself of the bag of golf sticks which the freshman now surrendered willingly, and led the way to the part of the platform where her companions had gathered around the three juniors.

"Here she is!" exclaimed Vera, as she approached. "Aha! Now I know why you left us all of a sudden!" She smiled winningly at Marjorie's companion, who allowed the barest flicker of a smile to touch her slightly pouting lips.

"Girls, I would like you to meet Miss——" Marjorie stopped, her color rising. The stranger had not volunteered her name at the time when Marjorie had introduced herself. She turned to the freshman with an apologetic smile. "Will you tell me your name?" she asked pleasantly.

"Oh, certainly. My name is Elizabeth Walbert." As she spoke her restless eyes began an appraisement of the group of girls whom Marjorie had addressed.

"Miss Walbert, this is Miss Mason, Miss Lynne, Miss Harper——" Marjorie presented her friends in turn to the newcomer, then said: "Please make Miss Walbert feel at home among us, while I greet our famous juniors."

"Oh, we knew you wouldn't forget your little friends," laughed Selma, "particularly the Swedish dwarf." Selma, who stood five feet nine, had bestowed this name upon herself, she being the tallest of the four girls who had chummed together since their enrollment at Hamilton.

Having warmly welcomed the trio, Marjorie realized Jerry was missing. She glanced quickly up
and down the platform in search of her. She finally
spied her coming down the platform with a plainly-
dressed girl whose pale face, under a brown sailor
hat, bore the unmistakable stamp of the student. In
one hand she carried a small black utility bag of
very shiny material. The other hand grasped the
handle of a large straw suitcase. Jerry carried the
mate to it. Her plump face registered nothing but
polite attention to what her companinon was saying. She was marching her freshman along, however, at a fair rate of speed. Not so far to their
rear the Sans had detrained. Their high-pitched
talk and laughter could be heard the length of the
platform, as they gathered up their luggage and
prepared to march on Hamilton. Jerry proposed to
be safely in the bosom of her friends with her find
before that march began.

"Come along, children. Let's be going. The
choo-choo cars are getting ready to choo-choo right
along to the next station. Look as I may, I see no
more arriving freshies—except the one Jeremiah is
now towing toward us." Leila added this as she
saw Jerry. "We'll delay our going in honor of the
freshie."

Next instant Jerry had joined them and was in-
troducing Miss Towne, of Omaha, Nebraska, as the

stranger had shyly declared herself. Amidst the
crowd of dainty, white-gowned girls, she looked not
unlike a dingy little brown wren. Miss Walbert
eyed her with growing disapproval and gave her a
perfunctory nod of the head. Immediately she
turned her attention to the on-coming Sans whom
she had already noticed. Her face brightened vis-
ibly as she watched them. While she had reluct-
antly decided that her new acquaintances were as
well dressed as she, and carried themselves as
though of social importance, their kindly reception
of a girl who was clearly a dig and a nobody displeased her. The very manner in which the other
group of girls were advancing made strong appeal
to her. They were more the type she had known at
Welden.

Marjorie felt an imperative tug at her arm.
"Who are those girls? They came from that private car. They are so much like my dear pals at
Welden." Elizabeth Walbert's babyish features
were alive with animation.

"They are juniors. I have met a few of them.
I can't really say that I have an acquaintance with
any of them." Marjorie could think of nothing
else to say of the Sans. She did not care to go into
detail regarding them.

"We go down those steps over there to reach the
yard where two of my friends have parked their

cars," she continued, with intended change of subject. Her companions were already moving toward the flight of stone steps. Miss Walbert still stood watching the approaching company of smartly-dressed girls.

"Pardon me. What did you say?" The absorbed freshman spoke without looking at Marjorie. "I think I have met one or two of those girls. Summer before last, at Newport, I met a Miss Myers and a Miss Stephens. We had quite a lot of fun together one afternoon at a tennis tournament. Yes, I am sure those are the same girls. I met them afterward at a dinner dance."

By this time the party had come within a few feet of where Marjorie and her annoying freshman find were standing. Marjorie felt the warm color flood her cheeks as a battery of unfriendly eyes was turned upon her. Her chums had already disappeared down the stairway, unaware that she had been left behind. She could hardly have conceived of a more disagreeable situation. Miss Walbert, however, was quite in her element. She had done precisely what she had intended to do.

"Excuse me, I must really speak to my friends. I'll probably go on to the college with them. Thank you so much."

With this Miss Walbert stepped hurriedly forward and addressed Joan Myers. "How do you

do? You are Miss Myers whom I met at the Newport tennis tournament, I believe. So surprised to
see you here and so pleased."

Joan Myers stared hard at the speaker before
replying. She recognized her as the girl she had
met at Newport on the occasion mentioned. She
also recalled the second meeting at the dance and
acted accordingly.

"How are you?" she returned affably, extending
her hand. "Of course I remember you. Strange
I can't recall your name. I met you at the Newport tournament and afterward at Mrs. Barry
Symonds' dance. Are you going to enter Hamilton? So pleased, I am sure. Won't you join our
party? You seem to be—er—well out of your
proper element." Joan added this with insulting
intent.

Marjorie had stepped back as Miss Walbert had
stepped forward. Her first impulse, in consideration of the cavalier dismissal she had received, had
been to turn and walk away. Courtesy prompted
her to wait a moment, thus making sure the freshman was accepted as an acquaintance by Joan Myers
and Harriet Stephens. She had barely turned away
as she heard Joan Myers say, "Won't you join our
party?" She could, therefore, hardly help hearing
the remark which followed.

She went without attempting even a farewell nod.

She was not hurt over the ill-bred manner in which she had been treated. She was disgusted with the other girl's uttter shallowness. She was also visited by a sense of dull disappointment. Hurrying to overtake her own party, she discovered she was still carrying the freshman's golf bag. In the annoyance of the moment she had forgotten all about it. Bravely she decided to return it at once and have it off her hands immediately. She was half way down the steps when she made this resolve. She quickly remounted the stairs. From the top step she could see the Sans, standing where she had left them. Four or five juniors whom she had seen on the platform before the train came in, were with them now.

"Is this the way to the station yard?" inquired a soft little voice at her elbow. "Can I get a taxi there that will take me to Hamilton College?"

Marjorie turned quickly to meet the questioning gaze of two velvety black eyes. The owner of the soft voice and black eyes was a girl no taller than Vera. She had a small, straight nose and a red bud of a mouth. Her hair, under the gray sports hat which matched her suit, was a blue black, so soft as to be almost feathery. As she surveyed the pretty stranger, Marjorie's recent pang of disappointment left her. Here, at least, was a freshman more after her own heart.

CHAPTER VII.

THE SANS' NEW RECRUIT.

"IF you will wait just a moment or two I will show you the way to the station yard. I am Marjorie Dean, of the sophomore class. I am down here today purposely to help incoming freshmen. I had one in tow a few minutes ago, but she met some acquaintances of hers and joined them. I carried off her golf bag and must return it. She is over there." Marjorie nodded toward the group. "Pardon me. I'll return instantly."

"Thank you, ever so much. I shall be glad to wait for you," sweetly responded the newcomer. "I am Barbara Severn, of Baltimore."

Marjorie stopped to acknowledge the introduction, then onerous as was the task, she went staunchly to it. Luckily for her, Miss Walbert stood at the edge of the group, momentarily neglected by her chosen acquaintances. They were busily engaged with their junior classmates.

"Here is your golf bag, Miss Walbert. I forgot

to give it to you when I left you." Her tone evenly
impersonal, it carried a note of reserve which the
other caught.

"Oh, thank you. I—that is—I forgot about it,
too." She attempted a smile as she reached out to
take it from Marjorie's hands.

"You are welcome." A slight inclination of the
head and Marjorie was gone.

Elizabeth Walbert watched the graceful figure in
white across the platform. Certainly this Dean girl
was awfully good style, she reflected.

"What did mamma's precious pet want with
you?" For the first time, since acknowledging an
introduction to Elizabeth, Leslie Cairns had condescended to address her.

"Nothing, except to return this. She carried it
and forgot to give it to me when I shook her. I am
glad she didn't wait and bring it over to Alston Terrace. I don't care much for that type of girl. She's
priggish and goody-goody, isn't she?" Miss Walbert promptly took her cue from Leslie.

While the babyish-looking freshman regarded
Leslie with a perfectly innocent expression, there
was lurking malice in her wide blue eyes. She had
not liked the dignity Marjorie had shown when
returning her property. It rankled in her petty
soul. With the gratitude of the proverbial serpent,

she was quite ready to sting the hand which had be-
friended her.

"I'll say she is," returned Leslie. "I can't endure
the sight of her and she knows it. You noticed she
did not stay long. Lucky you knew Joan and Harriet. I'd be sorry for you if you had been roped in
by that crowd of muffs." She laughed disagreeably.

"It would take more than that crowd of muffs,
as you call them, to rope me in," boasted the other
girl. "I saw at once they were not the kind that
make good pals. Not enough to them, you know.
Besides, I prefer not to be too friendly with a
stranger until I know her social position."

Leslie Cairns regarded her meditatively, then
held out her hand. "Shake hands on that," she
invited. "You seem to have some sense. I hope
you will stick to what you have said. If you do,
you may count yourself a friend of mine. You will
find, after you have been at Hamilton a while, that
my friendship amounts to a good deal."

"Oh, I am *sure* of that," emphasized the freshman. She was not sure at all. What she had
shrewdly taken stock of was the cut and material
of the English tweed sports suit Leslie was wearing.
It was a marvel of expense. It was conspicuous,
even among the smart traveling suits of her companions. So were her sports hat and English ties.
Leslie's assured manner also impressed her. She

decided that this exceedingly ugly but very "swagger" girl must be a person of importance at Hamilton.

Unmistakable gratification looked out from Leslie Cairns' roughly-chiseled features at the freshman's flattering response. Like the majority of the unworthy, she craved flattery. Since she had been denied physical beauty, she built her hopes on attracting admiration by her daring personality. During her freshman year at Hamilton she had acquired a certain kind of popularity by her high-handed methods. Possessed of an immense fortune, and in her own right, she had acquired tremendous power over her particular clique by reason of her money. Leslie never "went broke." The majority of the Sans received liberal allowances from home and spent them even more liberally. Leslie was a good port in time of storm—when she chose to be. Once under obligation to her, she was quite likely, if crossed, to let her debtor feel the weight of her displeasure.

"Did that Miss Dean have anything to say about us?" Leslie casually inquired. Finding herself admired, she preferred to cultivate her new acquaintance rather than devote her attention to those of her class who had come down to the train.

"She said—let me see." Miss Walbert knitted her light eyebrows in an elaborate effort at recollec-

tion. "She said she had never met any of you girls
and she didn't care for an acquaintance with you. I
I had asked who you were because I wanted so
much to know you. I recognized you girls at once
as my kind. Just to see your dandy crowd coming
along made me homesick for dear old Welden. I
palled with a crowd like that at prep."

"Our little angel, Miss Bean,—I always call her
Bean instead of Dean,—doesn't care what she does
with the truth," sneered Leslie. "Last fall we came
down to the train to meet her crowd. We knew
they were greenies from a little one-horse town
called Sanford. They were to be at the same
campus house as we. A few of us thought we
would try to help them. We took my friend, Miss
Weyman's, car and went to the station. Missed 'em
by about two minutes. They hired a taxi. We felt
mortified and went around to this Miss Dean's
room to apologize. We were almost frost-bitten.
They were so rude I felt ashamed for them. Afterward they started a lot of lies about us that made
trouble for us at the Hall."

"My goodness!" fluttered Miss Walbert. "I had
a narrow escape, didn't I? I will take pains to steer
clear of that whole crowd. I don't know whether I
would recognize most of them if I happened to meet
them on the campus. I would certainly know Miss
Dean."

"Where are you going to live?" Leslie dropped back into her usual indifferent drawl.

"Alston Terrace. I have an exam. in math. to try. I'm pretty sure of staying, though. Is Alston Terrace as nice as the house where you are? What did you say the name of your house was? Could I change and get in there?" There was suppressed eagerness in the last question.

"You could not." Leslie regarded the questioner with a superior smile. "I live at Wayland Hall. Our crowd live there, too. It's the best house on the campus, and hard to get into. It has two drawbacks; an idiot of a manager, and dear Miss Bean and her crowd. We have made complaint against the manager and she may have to go. She's a hateful old fossil and shows partiality. We can't do much about this crowd of which I've been telling you, unless they do something very malicious against us. Just let them start anything, though——" Her small black eyes narrowed unpleasantly.

At this juncture Natalie Weyman appealed to her to corroborate a statement she had just made to one of the juniors who had come down to the train to meet the Sans. Natalie had not been too busy with her friends to note that Leslie had condescended to show interest in the freshman. She, therefore, decided to break up the conversation going on between them. It was bad enough to have Lola Elster to contend with. She did not propose to allow this forward little snip, as she mentally characterized Miss Walbert, any leeway toward Leslie's favor which she could prevent.

"She doesn't like me and I don't like her," was the freshman's conclusion. When speaking to Leslie, Natalie had regarded her out of two very cold gray-blue eyes. The polite smile which had touched her lips was suggestive of frost.

It was the last thing needed to fire Elizabeth Walbert's ambition toward an intimate friendship with Leslie Cairns. She resolved that she would not only be chums with Leslie. Sooner or later she would take up her residence at Wayland Hall. She had always been clever at obtaining whatever she desired. To attain a residence at the Hall might not be so very difficult. At least it was worth the effort. She did not care who might be shoved out in order to make room for her.

Meanwhile Marjorie had safely conducted her second venture in freshmen to the spot where a knot of girls stood patiently awaiting her tardy appearance. Helen alone was missing, having gone into the town on an errand.

"Where were you? We thought you were right behind us. What has become of your blonde freshie? We knew something had happened," was the reception which greeted her and her charge.

"Do blondes change to brunettes in the twinkling of an eye?" laughed Leila, her blue eyes resting very kindly on Marjorie's pretty companion.

"They do not. Miss Walbert deserted me. She knew Miss Myers and Miss Stephens. She went with them." Marjorie made the explanation in a calm, level voice which did not invite present questioning.

"Then we can't count her in with this select aggregation," Vera said dryly. "Helen's gone, too, but her going was legitimate."

"Ah, well. We have gained one and lost one. Let us run off with our gain before someone happens along and coaxes her away from us. Might we not know her by name?" Leila turned to Marjorie with a wide ingratiating smile. The stranger was already regarding Leila with open amusement.

"You shall know her by name at once. You don't have to remind me to introduce her," retorted Marjorie. "I'll present you to her first of all. Miss Impatience, I mean Miss Harper, this is Miss Severn, of Baltimore." Marjorie again went through the ceremony of introduction, this time with smiles and whole-heartedness.

"We are thirteen in number, but who cares?" Leila announced. "Seven to one and six to the other car, Midget. As we aren't in the jitney business we won't come to blows over the one extra fare."

While they were disposing themselves in the two automobiles for the ride to Hamilton College, the sound of high-pitched voices announced the arrival on the scene of the Sans. Three of the juniors who had elected to meet them had driven their own cars to the station. Thus the illustrious Sans did not have to depend on the station's taxicabs.

While Leila would have liked to drive off in a hurry rather than encounter at such close range the girls she so heartily despised, she moved, instead, with the utmost deliberation. She was just climbing into the driver's seat when the small but noisy procession of young women came opposite to her car. Vera sat ready to start, her slender hands resting idly on the wheel as she waited for Leila's signal. The occupants of both cars, save for the freshman from Baltimore, were making a commendable effort to appear impersonal. Miss Severn, of Baltimore, was innocently interested in the newcomers from the fact that they were also students of Hamilton College.

Aside from considerable laughter, which sounded too pointed to be impersonal, the party of arriving juniors strolled past. Among the last came Leslie Cairns. She had insisted on walking with Elizabeth Walbert, greatly to Natalie's vexation. As she lounged past Leila's car she cast an insolent glance at the Irish girl. Leila returned it with an expression so inscrutably Celtic that Leslie hastily removed her gaze to Jerry, who sat beside Leila. She glared an intensity of ill-feeling at Jerry, which the latter longed to return, but did nothing worse than look blank.

Leila drove her car almost savagely around the station yard and out into the wide avenue. Sight of the Sans, particularly Leslie Cairns, had put her momentarily in a bad humor. Her virile Irish temperament forbade her to do other than love or hate with all her strength of being. She hated Leslie as energetically as she adored Marjorie.

"That Miss Walbert makes me sick," was Jerry's incensed comment as they bowled smoothly along the avenue. "I'd like to know just what happened to Marjorie. Of course she will tell us later. The idea of that little shrimp marching past us as though we were a collection of sign posts, particularly after we had treated her so decently. It's a good thing she showed her mettle from the start. Did you notice the way she snubbed my freshman?"

"I did. How, may I ask, do you happen to be out here with me instead of sitting faithfully in the tonneau beside your find?" quizzed Leila.

"Oh, Katherine and Lucy took her away from me. I guess I scared her. She is in Vera's car with them. If you don't enjoy my society, stop the buzz buggy and I will get out and walk. I may lose a pound or two, even if my feelings are hurt."

"It is here you'll stay. Tongue cannot tell how much I enjoy your society," Leila extravagantly assured. "I see you are liking the Sans a little less than ever. I am of the same mind. Did you see Leslie Cairns look at us; first at me, then you? I did not expect them back so soon. For all their private car they met with a tiny reception. Four or five juniors; that is quite different from two years ago."

"Maybe they've come back early to be on the scene and get a stand-in with the freshies," cannily suggested Jerry. "Wouldn't it be funny to see us and the Sans down at the station every day, grabbing the freshies as they came off the train, like a couple of jitney drivers?"

Leila laughed. "They will never go that far. That would take some kindness of heart and consideration. If they rushed the in-coming freshies just to spite us, they would soon sicken of their project. They are like the bandarlog in Kipling's Jungle books, they gather leaves only to throw them into the air."

"Some of them will take a trip up into the air this year if they don't mind their own affairs," threatened Jerry. "The freshman crop was small today. We garnered two and the Sans one. I suppose there were some others who were met by students besides ourselves. Marjorie thinks we ought to meet two trains a day, at least. The rest of our committee ought to be here. We could divide up the trains among us. You and Vera are really doing the work of the absent members."

"Say nothing about it. There is little to do this week. Vera and I were talking last night. We should have done this last year. We did not." Leila shrugged disapproval of her own former lack of interest in the welfare of other students.

"Leila," Marjorie leaned forward and called out, "Miss Severn is going to Acasia House. Do you know where Miss Towne is to go?"

"Somewhere off the campus," returned Leila. "Vera has her and her address. We are to take her to her boarding place first."

Miss Towne's boarding house turned out to be a modest two-story brick house about half a mile off the campus. It was one of a scattered row, there being only a few houses in the immediate vicinity of the college. Muriel and Katherine helped her to the door with her luggage. Her friendly escort called her a cordial good-bye from the automobiles, after promising to look her up as soon as she should be fairly settled. She went to her new quarters in a daze of sheer happiness, feeling much as Cinder-

ella must have when she unexpectedly found a fairy
God-mother.

Acasia House being Miss Severn's destination,
the two cars wound their way in and out of the
beautiful campus driveway. At the center drive
they separated, Vera taking her car straight to
Wayland Hall on account of Selma, Nella and Hortense. Muriel went with them, declining to be
parted from her recently regained room-mate.

Leila drove slowly toward Acasia House, endeavoring to give their freshman charge full opportunity to see the campus in its early autumn glory.
Brimming with eager enthusiasm, Marjorie pointed
out the various halls, the library, the chapel and the
campus houses. She was pleased to find her freshman no less enthusiastic than herself over the
campus itself. Marjorie took that as another good
sign. No one who was really sincere at heart could
fail to be impressed by the campus.

CHAPTER VIII.

HER FATHER'S METHODS.

"THERE is just one thing about it. We have *got* to get busy." Leslie Cairns made this announcement with special emphasis on the word "got." Her face wore an expression of sullen determination. "Those Sanford goody-goodies are out to do us."

"Out to do us?" repeated Natalie Weyman, with questioning inflection. "What do you mean, Les? I failed to see any particular triumph on their part this afternoon. They merely marched off with a seedy-looking freshie or two. No one we wanted." Natalie shrugged her disdain of the Lookouts' capture. Too bad that simple-acting Walbert creature didn't stay with dear Miss Bean. We could live without her. I have no use for that girl."

Leslie's eyes narrowed. She banged her dessert spoon on the table with a vicious clang and thrust her chin forward.

"Probably *you* haven't, Miss Jealousy," she

sneered. "I fail to see anything simple about Miss Walbert. She has three times as much sense as certain persons I could name."

"Meaning me, I suppose." Natalie's tone was equally sneering. She was white with anger, principally at having been called "Miss Jealousy." Leslie had often privately accused her of being jealous-hearted. This was the first time she had ever taunted her so openly of it.

"Won't you two *please* stop scrapping?" begged Margaret Wayne in a tired voice. "I thought we came to the Colonial for a pleasant evening. It has been anything but that, with you two snarling back and forth at each other like a couple of tigers at the Zoo."

"Much obliged for the compliment," flung back Natalie in frost-bitten accents.

"Oh, you are entirely welcome." Margaret laid provoking stress on the "welcome."

"Looks as if the scrap might be trusted to you, Wayne. You certainly can hold up your end of it." Leslie called her friends by their last names merely to be insolent. "Anyone can fuss with Nat, you know. She has the sweet disposition of a very sour pickle most of the time."

"Since that is your opinion of me, I am surprised you ever cared to be friends with me at all." Very near to tears, Natalie managed to preserve an offended dignity which had more effect upon Leslie than any sarcastic retort might have had. Nor was Natalie unaware of this. Momentarily angered, she had made a strenuous effort to choke back the biting words just behind her lips. She always remembered one cold fact in time. It never paid in the long run to quarrel with Leslie.

"Oh, you are not so bad when one has grown used to you, Leslie patronizingly conceded. "Excuse me for losing my temper and telling you the plain truth about yourself."

Natalie's color rose. She hated Leslie's patronizing insolence more than she hated her open vituperation. She would have liked to say that she was amazed to learn that Leslie ever told the plain truth about anything. Prudence warned her to let the quarrel drop.

"I accept your apology, Leslie," she said with great sweetness, entirely ignoring the sting of Leslie's remarks.

"What?" Leslie stared. A faint snicker arose from two or three of the other girls. "You seem to have recovered your wits again, Nat," she said with elaborate carelessness. We are quits, I guess, for the present."

"Thank goodness!" This from Joan Myers. "Now that peace has been restored, perhaps you will condescend to tell us what you started out to say, Leslie."

"De-lighted." Leslie bowed ironically. "To jump into the middle of the subject at once, I asked you seven Sans to this party tonight for a purpose. We eight girls are the founders of the Sans. I told all the other Sans that I wasn't going to ask them here tonight, and not to get their backs humped about it. I promised 'em a big party at the Ivy Saturday night. There is a private dining room there with a long table that will seat the whole eighteen of us. I don't know whether they liked it or not, and I don't care. It was up to us to talk things over and let them into it afterward."

"Some of the girls had other engagements anyway," put in Joan Myers. "I know Anne Dawson and Loretta Kelly were invited to a senior blow-out at Alston Terrace."

"Well, that's neither here nor there," retorted Leslie somewhat rudely. It did not please her to learn that any of the Sans had received more attention from the seniors than herself. Thus far she had not been the recipient of an invitation to dine from a senior. She was still inwardly sore at the lack of attention they had met with on their arrival at Hamilton station.

"I don't think it is a very good policy for we eight founders of the Sans to keep to ourselves too much," deprecated Dulcie Vale, regardless of Leslie's views on the subject. "The whole eighteen of us will have to stick together and work hard if we expect to keep the upper hand of things here at Hamilton."

"Oh, forget it," ordered Leslie brusquely. "Your trouble is easy to explain. You are sore because I didn't invite Eleanor, your pal, to this dinner."

"I am not," stoutly contradicted Dulcie. Nevertheless her sudden flush belied her words.

"Of course you are," went on Leslie imperturbably. "Understand, I didn't *want* the rest of the gang here tonight, and that's that. What I started out to say when Nat and Joan and Margaret and you butted in, one by one, was this: We must bestir ourselves and make a fuss over the freshies. This year's freshman class is, I'm told, the largest entering class for ten years. I don't feel like bothering myself with the diggy, priggy element of freshies, but even they will have to be considered. I'd do anything to spite that Sanford crowd and upset the progress they have made against us."

"What progress have they made, I'd like to know?" demanded Harriet Stephens scornfully. "If you mean the way they got back at us for ragging Miss Dean, I think that was *simply disgraceful* in them to call a meeting as they did and blacken our standing at Wayland Hall. It is a wonder we managed to keep our rooms at the Hall after all the row they made about a little bit of ragging."

"We kept them, just the same, and you may thank Joan and I for it," significantly reminded Leslie. "I know old Remson is so sore at us she could snap our heads off. The funny part of it is, she will never know how cleverly we blocked her little game. That reminds me. I don't want the rest of the Sans to know the way we worked that scheme. Eight of us in the secret is enough. Remember, if it ever got out we would be all through at Hamilton College."

"Do you believe we would be expelled, Les?" asked Dulcie Vale, looking worried.

"I don't believe it. I *know* we would. Nothing could save us. Never mind being scared, though. No one will ever know the rights of our plot unless some one of you girls here is silly enough to tell it. That's why I am cautioning you to be careful."

"Leslie is precisely right about that," Natalie Weyman hastened to agree. "We shall have to be very careful what we do this year. I think that a little missionary work among the freshies would be a good thing for all of us. Later on we can drop them if they grow to be too much of a bore."

"They will take care of themselves as they get used to college," predicted Leslie. "If some of 'em turn out to be really smart, like Lola Elster, for instance, then we needn't be slow about running with them. *You* think, Nat, that I have a crush on that Miss Walbert." Leslie turned directly to Natalie. "I have not. She is just the person I need, though, to carry out a plan of mine. Joan and Harriet both say that the Walberts have millions. They have a wonderful place at Newport. So Mrs. Barry Symonds told Joan. What did you say the Walbert's place was called, Joan?"

"Evermonde," furnished Joan promptly. "I was sorry I didn't go and call on the kid, particularly after I found out who she was. I only met her twice at the tag end of the season."

"What I want her for," continued Leslie with slow emphasis, "is the freshman presidency."

"Some modest little ambition," murmured Evangeline Heppler.

"Um-m! Well, rather!" agreed Adelaide Forman. "How do you propose to make it happen, Les?"

"Leave that to me. I'm not prepared to tell you yet. I only know that it has to happen. It will give us a good hold on the freshies" Leslie's looselipped mouth tightened perceptibly. "We'll have to do some clever electioneering. I expect it will cost money. I don't care how much it costs, so long as I win my point."

"You mean we must rush the freshies?" interrogated Margaret Wayne.

"Yes," nodded Leslie. "Cart them around in our cars. Blow them off to dinners and luncheons. Begin tomorrow to go down to the station and grab them as they come off the train."

"Deliver me from the station act." Joan Myers made a wry face.

"You'll have to go to it with the rest of us," insisted Leslie with a suggestive lowering of brows. "This is really serious business, Joan. I don't intend to sit still and see a bunch of muffs like those Sanford girls run Hamilton College. We had things all our own way until they came upon the scene. Nothing has been as it should be for us since then. They have turned a lot of upper class girls against us. I don't mean Leila Harper and her crowd. They never had any time for us. There are a good many Silverton Hall girls of our social standing, but they went almost solid against us in that Miss Reid affair last year. Who was to blame for that? Those Sanford busybodies, you may be sure."

"I believe it was that Miss Page who started the Silverton Hall gang," differed Dulcie Vale, with a touch of sulkiness. She was still peeved at Leslie and now delighted in expressing a contrary opinion.

"I don't care what *you* believe," mimicked Leslie

disagreeably. "I say it was the Sanford crowd who started the trouble."

"Say it, then. Sing it if you like," retorted Dulcie. "I am privileged to my own opinion."

"Keep it to yourself, then. I don't care to hear it," coolly returned Leslie. "You girls make me weary. You are all so ready to start fussing over nothing."

"You are just as ready!" burst forth Dulcie, in a sudden gust of anger. "You think we all ought to do precisely as you say and never have an opinion of our own. I fail to see why I, at least, should be bossed by you. It isn't we girls that are at fault. It is you. I like you, Leslie, when you don't try to run everything. When you begin bullying, I can't endure you. Please don't attempt to bully me, for I won't stand it."

"There is one thing about it," broke in Harriet Stephens decidedly, "we shall not accomplish much if there is no unity among us. So far as I am concerned, I would rather have Leslie take the lead. I will never forgive the Sanford crowd for what they did to us last March. If Leslie can find ways to get even with them, I am willing to do as she says, simply to see those hateful girls defeated in whatever they set out to do."

"That is the proper spirit," approved Leslie. "Believe me, I know what I am saying when I tell

you that we must fight those girls and put them in
the background where they belong. The way to
begin this year is to win over the freshies. The
minute it is known we are interesting ourselves in
these greenies' welfare, our popularity will take a
jump upward. Every one of you can either give me
your promise tonight to help or keep away from me
the rest of the year. Think it over. Don't promise
and then go to grumbling behind my back about it.
If you do, I'll be sure to hear it."

"It will be rather good fun to play angel to the
freshies for a change," said Evangeline Hepper.
"We might have a picnic some Saturday, or give a
hop for them. Have it understood, of course, that
it was the Sans Soucians who were to be the hostesses."

"We can decide better what to do after we have
met a few of the freshmen," returned Leslie. "I
hope there won't be many of those beggarly-look-
ing girls who come into college on scholarships or
scrape their way through without a cent above their
expenses. They are so tiresome. That Miss Langly,
of our class, is a glowing example of what I mean."

"She is very high and mighty since the Sanford
crowd took her up, isn't she?" shrugged Natalie.

"She always was, for that matter," said Adelaide
Forman. "Those girls have praised her and babied

her until she is a good deal more infatuated with herself than she used to be."

"That is another reason I have for wanting to get back at them," asserted Leslie. "You all know the snippy way she acted when we asked her to change rooms with Lola. Worse still, she had to go and tell her troubles to the Sanford crowd. They started right in to tell everyone how brilliant she was and how shabbily we had treated her. Then the Silverton Hall girls took it up and spread the news abroad that Langly had won a scholarship no one else had been able to win for twenty years. That sent her stock away up and we had to stop ragging her or be disliked. I shall not forget that little performance in a hurry."

"They certainly put one over on us with that miserable old beauty contest, too." Natalie's voice quivered with bitterness.

"Leila Harper was to blame for that, Nat. She is the cleverest girl at Hamilton. We made a serious mistake in the beginning about her. They say her father has oodles of money." Joan looked brief regret at the mistake the Sans had made in not cultivating Leila.

"We never could have got along with her," Leslie said decidedly. "I am glad we never took her up. I detest her and Vera Mason, too, but not half so hard as I do Miss Bean and her satellites." Leslie invariably said "Bean" instead of Dean in derision of Marjorie.

She now paused, her heavy features dark with resentment. The independence of Marjorie Dean and her friends was a thorn to her flesh. Each time she had attempted to injure them she had been ingloriously defeated. She was determined, this year, not only to win back and maintain her former leadership at Hamilton College, but also to crush the rising power of the girls she so greatly disliked.

"Are you going to let the rest of the Sans in on this station business?" inquired Harriet Stephens.

"Naturally; we need them to help us out. Don't get the idea I am trying to keep the other girls out of our plans. I am not. It's like this. The eight of us ran around together at prep school before we took the rest of the girls into our crowd. We have always been a little more confidential among ourselves because we are the old guard, as you might say. Of course they know all about our troubles with Miss Bean and her pals. They went through them with us. What we must keep to ourselves is this Wayland Hall affair. We saved their rooms for them. They know that. They don't need to know the exact process by which we did it, do they? I merely told them that I thought I could get my father to fix up matters if there was any trouble started. They let us do all the worrying over it. I guess we have the right to keep it to ourselves. That settles you, Dulcie. You can quit sulking because I won't allow you to tell everything you know to Eleanor. Remember it is to your own precious interest not to."

Leslie delivered herself of this long speech very much as her father might have addressed himself to a group of his business lieutenants. It was received with a certain amount of respect which was always accorded her by her chums when she adopted her father's tone and manner. They were all still more or less uneasy over the method which she and Joan had employed to save them their residence at Wayland Hall.

"Leslie, do you think we will ever have any trouble about—well—about what you and Joan did?" questioned Evangeline Heppler rather uneasily.

"Not unless you let someone outside this crowd into the secret. The only other person who knows it would not dare tell it. She would deny knowing a thing about it to the very end. Don't worry. That is past. It won't come up again. We are safe enough. It is up to us now to put the enemy on the back seats where they belong and regain the ground we lost last year. I repeat what I said awhile ago. We have *got* to get busy."

CHAPTER IX.

FRESHIE FISHING.

THE result of Leslie Cairns' rallying of her companions to her standard was made manifest when a fairly lengthy procession of automobiles, driven by Sans sped along the smooth roads to the station on the following Friday morning.

While Leslie was not at all on good terms with Miss Humphrey, the registrar, she had other sources of information open to her regarding college matters which were by rights none of her affairs. It was, therefore, easy for her to learn how many of the freshman class had registered and govern herself accordingly. With the tactics of a general she went the rounds of the Sans, ordering them to be on hand all day Friday with their cars, provided these highly useful machines in the campaign had arrived on the scene. At least half of the Sans were already in possession of their own pet cars, these having been driven to Hamilton by the chauffeurs of their respective families. Nine automobiles accordingly went to swell the procession that sunny Friday morning and the Sans were in high feather as, two to a car, they set out on their self-imposed welcoming task.

Leslie had decreed that they were to meet every incoming train of importance that day and spare no pains to make themselves agreeable to the newcomers. In case the freshman yield was small, they were to use their judgment about being friendly with returning students of the upper classes.

"If we can't fill our cars with freshies, you girls all know just about who's who at Hamilton. Don't pick up a soph, junior or senior unless you are sure that it will be to our advantage to do so. Keep an eye out for faculty. Nothing like being on the soft side of them."

Such was Leslie's counsel to her followers who were entering the campaign with a malicious zest infinitely gratifying to her. While the other eight cars contained two occupants apiece, Leslie's pet roadster held a third passenger. Leslie had elected to invite Elizabeth Walbert to share the roadster with herself and Harriet Stephens. This was not in the least to Natalie Weyman's liking. Her own car having arrived, she was obliged to drive it. She had not emerged from her cloud of resentment against the officious Miss Walbert, nor was she likely to.

Meanwhile the faithful little committee, truly devoted to freshman welfare, was blissfully unaware that their duties were about to be snatched from them by the predatory Sans. The absent members of the committee having arrived, the seven girls held a meeting on Thursday evening in Marjorie's room, dividing the trains to be met among them. Marjorie and Jerry were to be reinforced by Leila and Vera. The others had also certain friends among the sophs, juniors and seniors who could be relied upon to help them.

Marjorie and Jerry having been detailed to meet the ten-twenty train from the west each morning, Vera and Leila never failed to be on hand with their cars by nine o'clock. This permitted of a delightful spin in the fresh air over the many picturesque drives in the vicinity of Hamilton College. Always punctual, Leila never failed to get them to the station in plenty of time for the train.

Driving into the station yard on this particular Friday morning, the sight of a line of shining automobiles caused them to blink in momentary astonishment.

"The Sans!" muttered Leila, giving vent to her usual whistle of surprise. "Now what are the heathen up to? Look at that line of cars! Almost every color except violet. What do you make of that?"

"They must expect a delegation of their own friends," guessed Marjorie. "A lot of upper class girls are expected at Hamilton today."

"Freshies, too," added Leila, as she brought her car to a stop and prepared to alight. "Miss Humphrey told me she thought a large part of the freshman class would be in on Friday and Saturday. I was complaining to her of how few we had landed in the past week."

By this time Jerry and Vera were both out of Vera's car and had come quickly up to Marjorie and Leila.

"Can you beat it?" saluted Jerry. "We think the Sans have come freshie fishing. What do you think?"

"Little Miss Charitable thinks they may be down here to meet their own friends," remarked Leila with a mischievous glance toward Marjorie. "You guileless infant! Don't you know what has happend? The Sans are going to do just what some of us said the other night they wouldn't take the trouble to do. They have gone into the welcoming business."

"One, two, three——" Vera had begun to count

the colorful array of automobiles. "Nine machines." She turned to Leila with a little laugh. "It shows which way the wind is blowing, doesn't it?"

"We are going to have some fun with them this year," predicted Leila with a touch of grimness. "They are beginning to be afraid of losing their glory or you would never see them down here welcoming freshmen."

"Let's get along and take a look at our rivals," suggested Jerry humorously. "I suppose they will all be dressed to kill. Too bad they can't appear in full evening dress. That would be so much more impressive."

"I am not going to let them bother me," announced Marjorie placidly. "The kind of girls we are specially on the lookout to help will not be their kind. They will pick out the smartly-dressed ones and leave the humble ones, if there are any, to us. After all, there are not very many poor students at Hamilton. I suppose it is because of the high tuition fees and the expensive board here."

"We had better hustle along. Hear that?" Jerry raised a hand for attention. "That is the train whistling."

Without further delay the quartette hurriedly sought the stairs and reached the platform a moment or two before the train appeared in sight.

"I shall not be sorry when our committee duties end," Marjorie said with a faint sigh. "It seems as though about all I have done since I came back to Hamilton is to meet trains. I have a lot of things to do for myself that I haven't had time to think about. I haven't arranged my study programme either."

"Cheer up. Tomorrow will end it," consoled Vera. "There will be some stragglers next week, of course, but today and Saturday will see the most of the students here."

"Look at the Sans." Leila arched her brows and drew down the corners of her mouth. "Hmm! Posted all along the platform with General Cairns in the most prominent place. And do my eyes tell me lies! Isn't that girl hanging on her arm the freshie you lost the other day, Marjorie?"

"Yes, it is Miss Walbert." Marjorie instantly identified the fickle freshman.

"You never said a word to any of us about what happened the other day except that she knew Miss Myers and left you," Jerry said. "I meant to ask you about her afterward and I forgot it. Was she snippy with you?"

"No-o; not exactly snippy." A faint smile rose to Marjorie's lips. "She wasn't satisfied to stay with us. The minute she caught sight of the Sans she wanted to be with them. Then she found she knew Miss Myers and Miss Stephens, and she simply walked off and left us."

"She's a first-class snob, isn't she?" persisted Jerry.

"Yes, she is," Marjorie responded truthfully. "Frankly I am not sorry she left us. I seldom dislike a girl on sight, but I did not like her. I found it hard work to be polite to her. There was something about her that jarred on me dreadfully."

The arrival of the train cut off further conversation for the moment. The four girls turned their attention to watching the little stream of girls that issued from the several cars. Greatly to their amusement the Sans behaved somewhat after the manner of taxicab drivers eagerly soliciting fares.

"We stand small chance with the freshies today, unless we can line up beside the Sans and call out our merits," laughed Leila.

Marjorie smiled absently, only half hearing Leila's remark. Her eyes were roving up and down the platform in an effort to pick up any girl whom the Sans might deliberately choose to overlook. She saw no one. The considerable number of girls who had descended the car steps were being taken in tow by the new self-constiuted reception committtee. The clanging of bells and the sharp blast of the whistle proclaimed the train to be ready to move on. The Sans and their finds were already turning their back upon it.

Several yards below where she was standing, Marjorie suddenly spied a lithe, girlish figure coming down the car steps almost at a run, burdened though she was by a traveling bag and a suitcase. At the bottom step she lost her grip on the leather bag and it rolled onto the platform. Instantly Marjorie hurried to her, followed by Jerry. Leila and Vera were genially shaking hands with two seniors who were also behind the main body of the crowd in leaving the train.

"Oh!" exclaimed a dismayed voice, as the traveler's feet found the solid platform.

Marjorie had already recovered the leather bag. Nor was she a second too soon. Joan Myers had lagged behind her companions to talk to a senior who had just come off the train. She had also seen the solitary arrival. She had not failed to note the girl's ultra smart appearance and consequently decided to take charge of her. Utterly ignoring the fact that Marjorie had retrieved the rolling grip, Joan grandly held out her hand to the newcomer.

"Freshman?" she inquired, in sweet tones. "So glad to welcome you to Hamilton. Do let me help you. A number of my friends and myself are making a point of welcoming freshman arrivals. Just come with me and I will see that you are taken care of."

Forgetful for the fraction of an instant of the gracious rôle she was essaying, Joan flashed Marjorie a contemptuous glance. It said more plainly than words: "You are not wanted here."

Well aware of it, Marjorie stood her ground. She was still in possession of the bag. Joan's interruption had given her no time either to greet the traveler or return her property.

"Thank you. I am expecting a cousin of mine to meet me." The girl responded courteously, but with a trace of reserve. "Perhaps you know her. She is Miss Page of Silverton Hall."

"I know who she is. I believe I have met her." A dull tide of red mounted to Joan's cheeks. "So long as you are to be met by *her* I won't intrude. So pleased to have met you, I'm sure." With this hasty and insincere assurance, Joan beat a rapid retreat, leaving Marjorie, Jerry and the freshman to their own devices.

"I don't believe she can be a very intimate friend of Robin's," calmly commented the girl, a slightly mocking light in her pretty blue eyes.

"She isn't," was Jerry's blunt answer, "but we are. If you are willing to take our word for it, we shall be glad to see you to Hamilton College. I heard yesterday that Robin was back, but we haven't seen her yet. I am Geraldine Macy and this is my friend Marjorie Dean."

"I have heard of both of you from Robin. I spent two weeks with her at Cape May this summer. Now I know I am in the hands of friends. Tell you the truth, I didn't like that other girl a little bit. I hadn't the least intention of toddling along with her. I was glad I had Robin for an excuse. I really thought she would meet me. As you haven't seen her since you heard she was back, that means she certainly isn't around here now. I think that tall, red-faced girl was awfully rude to thrust herself upon me when she could plainly see that you were holding my bag." She now addressed herself to Marjorie.

"I made up my mind to hang on to the bag until I had a chance to speak to you." Marjorie evaded passing opinion on Joan. "Jerry and I are on committee to welcome freshmen. This morning a crowd of juniors came down to the station for that purpose. We did not have any luck freshie-fishing. The juniors caught them all, with the exception of yourself."

"I came near being carried on to the next station," laughed the girl. "I dropped my coin purse and couldn't find it. I was frantic, for I had stuffed some bank notes into it and naturally didn't want to leave the train without it. It had rolled

under the seat just in front of me. By the time I
found it the train was ready to start and I had to
hustle. I nearly took a fall on that last step, but
saved myself by letting my bag go instead of me.
Oh, I forgot to introduce myself. I am Phyllis
Marie Moore, at your service, and when we all get
past the Miss stage you may like to call me Phil.
I used to be a terrible tomboy until I grew up. I
am a rapid fire talker. I love to talk and I have
very strong likes and dislikes. Let me see. Oh,
yes. I say outright whatever I think, whether it
sets well or not. Those are the main points about
me, I guess. You may now discard me or take me
to your heart; just as you please," she ended with
a merry little laugh.

"We shall be delighted to begin cherishing you
immediately," Marjorie gaily assured.

Jerry was quick to add to the assurance. Given
also to very positive likes and dislikes, she had
already taken a great fancy to Robin's lively cousin.
She had a shrewd opinion that it would not take
Phillis Marie Moore long to make a prominent
place for herself in the freshman class.

Leila and Vera now joined them, in company
with the two seniors, who were going to the campus
in Vera's car. Leila claimed the privilege of conveying the freshman arrival at Silverton Hall, her
destination. Once there, Miss Moore's three upper

class guardians were given a vociferous greeting by a bevy of jubliant girls.

"You bad old goose!" was Robin Page's affectionate censure as she hugged her tall, boyish cousin. "Why didn't you wire me?"

"I did," returned Phyllis. "You'll probably receive it tomorrow. That will be so nice, won't it, to get a wire that I am on the way when I'm already here?"

"You fell into good hands, anyway," Robin beamed on the trio of Wayland Hall girls. "Do you notice anything different about me?" she asked anxiously of them all. Very carefully she turned her head so that the small knot of hair at the nape of her white neck could be seen. "I am a real grown-up young person now!" she proudly exclaimed. "I can do up my hair."

"You are that," Leila agreed in her most gallant Irish manner. "It is now that we shall have to begin to treat you with proper respect."

"See that you do," retorted Robin. "Right away quick I am going to treat you folks to luncheon. You must stay. It will be ready in a few minutes. Come up to my room and we can hold an impromptu reception until the bell rings. The Silvertonites are all anxious to see you. As sophs we have a duty to perform. We must try hard to impress my freshman cousin. Do telephone Ronny,

Lucy, Muriel and Vera to come over. You can run 'em over in your car, Leila, in a jiffy."

"Many thanks for Vera's and my invitation. We can't accept, for we have a luncheon engagement at Baretti's with two seniors. I must be hurrying along or I'll be late. I'll send the girls back in my car. Any of them can drive it."

Leila took hurried farewell of her friends and drove off at top speed. True to her word, it was not long before her car swung into sight again driven by Ronny. The three new arrivals were received with the same heartiness which had been extended to Marjorie and Jerry. By the time they appeared, Robin's large square room was overflowing with girls.

Once more in the genial atmosphere which always pervaded Silverton Hall, the petty worries and annoyances of the past week fell away from Marjorie. She entertained a momentary regret that she had not chosen Silverton Hall as a residence in the beginning. She and her chums would have found life so much pleasanter there.

Then the face of kind little Miss Remson rose before her. She realized how very fond she had grown of the upright, sorely-tried manager. She reflected, too, that, if the Lookouts had not gone to Wayland Hall to live, it would have been much harder for Katherine Langly. Neither would she have known Leila, Vera, or Helen Trent intimately. Besides, she loved Wayland Hall and its beautiful premises best of all the campus houses. It had been Brooke Hamilton's favorite house. Miss Remson had once told her this. In spite of the difficulties the Lookouts had encountered at the Hall, Marjorie wondered if, perhaps, they had not gravitated to it for some beneficient, hidden purpose which only time might reveal.

CHAPTER X.

WINNING OVER THE FRESHMEN.

As Vera had predicted, Saturday brought to Hamilton a goodly number of freshmen. Though the faithful reception committee was strictly on duty that day, the Sans relieved them of a large part of their conscientious task. They were even more in evidence than on Friday. Greatly to the surprise of Marjorie and her companions, they laid themselves out to be democratic. They rushed every young woman who bore freshman earmarks with a zeal which might have been highly commendable had it been sincere. Out of the considerable number of freshman arrivals that Saturday, Marjorie and her committee captured not more than half a dozen.

"The end of a perfect day, I don't think," grumbled Jerry. The five-fifty train had come and gone. Though the seven sophomores had all been on duty, not one of them had a freshman to show for it.

"I'm glad it is over," Marie Peyton said wearily,

as the nine disgusted workers strolled to their waiting cars. "I suppose the Sans thought we would contest the ground with them. I wouldn't be so ill-bred. Come on over to the Colonial for dinner. I hereby invite you. We need a little pleasant recreation to offset this fiasco. Next year, no committee duty for me. I have had enough of it."

"How many freshies do you think they have captured altogether?" asked Blanche Scott.

"Oh, sixty or seventy, at least," was Elaine Hunter's guess. "They have been down to every train for the last two days. Between trains they have hung around the Ivy and that other tea shop just below it. I don't recall the name. It opened only last week."

"The Lotus," supplied Jerry. "The funny part of it is the way Miss Cairns has marched that Miss Walbert around with her. They seem to be very chummy.

"Leslie Cairns is trying to popularize Miss Walbert with the freshmen. That is why she has been keeping her on hand at all the trains. I am sure of it," stated Vera positively. "You just watch and see if I am not right. The Sans are going to try to run the freshman class. Otherwise they would never have gone to the trouble they have."

"They won't keep it up. Mark what I tell you,

there will be a lot of snubbed and very wrathful freshies before the month is out," prophesied Leila.

"I hope the grand awakening comes before their class election. I doubt it. With Miss Walbert as president of 19——, the Sans would feel they had really put one over on us. I think Phyllis Moore, Robin's cousin, would make a fine freshman president." Jerry glanced about her for corroboration.

"Why not do some quiet electioneering for her, then," suggested Grace Dearborn. "It is just as fair for us to boost a freshie for an office as for the Sans. It would be only a helpful elder sister stunt. We need not make ourselves prominent. A girl like Miss Moore would be a fine influence to her class. This Miss Walbert would not be."

"It isn't really our business," demurred Marjorie, "but I think it would be a good thing, nevertheless. We are fighting for democracy. The Sans are fighting for popularity and false power. I am willing to do all I can to help the cause along. I know Ronny and Muriel and Lucy will feel the same. Jerry's here to speak for herself."

The others agreeing to enter into a quiet little plot to put the right girl in the freshman presidential chair, how they should go about it formed the main topic of conversation at Marie's dinner at the quaint Colonial that evening. All sorts of ways and means were suggested, only to be abandoned.

It was impossible to proceed until they had come
into more of a knowledge of the freshmen themselves. Each, however, pledged herself to make a
point of getting acquainted with the freshmen in
the house where she resided and sounding them on
their policies, with a view toward giving them a
hint in the right direction.

It seemed to Marjorie that the next few days following her strenuous service on committee were
days of undiluted peace. Busy with her study programme she forgot, for the time being, that there
ever were any such persons as the Sans Soucians.
She had decided on French, chemistry, Greek trag-
edy, Horace's odes and spherical trigonometry for
the fall term, a programme that meant hard study.
Since coming to Hamilton her active interest in
chemistry had increased and she planned to carry
the study of it through her entire college course.
The laboratory at Sanford High School had been
well equipped, but the Hamilton laboratories were
all that scientific progress could devise. Marjorie
hailed her chemistry hours with the keenest pleasure.

The other four Lookouts were hardly less occupied than herself in arranging their college affairs
for the fall term. With a year of college behind
them it was much easier to buckle down to study
and enjoy it than it had been when they had first
entered Hamilton. Girl-like, they loved the good

times college offered, yet they were as quick to appreciate the rare educational advantages Hamilton afforded and make the most of them. The average college girl takes the utmost pride in keeping to the fore in her studies. In this the Lookouts were no exception.

Not forgetting their pledge to get acquainted speedily with the freshmen in their own house, the Lookouts found themselves completely blocked in their well-meant design by the Sans. To begin with, there were only four freshmen at Wayland Hall. These the Sans completely monopolized. As yet, no one at the Hall outside the Sans had a speaking acquaintance with them.

Silverton Hall was also at a disadvantage by reason of the few vacancies there. It had been almost entirely a freshman house the previous year. It was now practically sophomore. A few girls, having made changes on account of friends in other houses, there had been eight vacancies and no more. Phyllis Moore had been fortunate enough to secure board there. The seven other freshmen had turned out to be delightful girls with no snobbish notions. Seven democrats in a class of one hundred ten, with the politics of the other hundred and two doubtful, did not point to a speedy election of Phyllis to the freshman presidency.

"We might as well give up boosting Phil as a

hopeless job," Jerry remarked to Marjorie one evening, as the two girls were putting away their books preparatory to retiring. Both made it a rule not to talk over outside matters until next day's recitations had been prepared. "It is two weeks since we planned the fateful boost and none of us have made much headway."

"I know it." Marjorie looked up regretfully from the scattered sheets of the finished theme which she was collecting. "The trouble is, so many of the freshies are at Alston Terrace. Acasia House has about twenty. Ethel Laird says they are a fairly affable set, but Miss Burton and Miss Elster are doing their best to spoil them. There are as many as twenty-five freshies off the campus entirely. Miss Humphrey told me that. There were twelve registrations from the town of Hamilton this year. Of course those students go home after recitations."

"Not much can be done when a class is so scattered. I mean by us. Let me count 'em up. There are twenty-five off the campus, eight at Silverton Hall," enumerated Jerry; "four here, forty-four at Alston Terrace. Think of that. That makes one hundred and one. Now where are the other nine? At Craig Hall, perhaps, or Houghton House. You see Miss Walbert has the advantage over Phil as she is at Alston Terrace, the freshie center."

Marjorie nodded. "It doesn't look very promising for Phil," she said. "Robin would love to have Phil win the presidency. She is so proud of her. The Silverton Hall crowd adore her already. She is a dear. She is so full of fun. I like her frank, boyish ways. Leila told me today that the Sans are planning some kind of party for the freshmen. She heard it somewhere on the campus. I don't know who told her."

"That is to taffy the freshmen so they will vote for Miss Walbert," was Jerry's instant uncharitable conclusion. "They haven't held their class election yet. When is this party to be, I wonder?"

"Leila doesn't know. If the Sans do make a party for the freshmen I doubt if all of them will attend it. It won't be at all like the regular freshman dance. Still," she continued reflectively, "if the Sans take that much trouble for them, they ought to respond."

"Yes; I guess that's so. The freshies haven't been here long enough to know the charming Sans as they really are. In their infant verdancy they will probably look upon it as a great honor. They'll probably be more enlightened after they have attended it," Jerry added with a wicked little grin.

Two days later it became circulated about the campus that the freshmen had been invited by the Sans to attend a picnic, instead of a party, to be given at Pine Crest, a wooded height about five

miles east of Hamilton College. For many years it
had been a favorite college picnic ground. Hardly
a Saturday passed, when the weather was good,
without an invasion, great or small, of its fragrant,
pine-shaded premises. It was an ideal spot for an
al fresco luncheon. As it could be reached by automobile, it was all the more popular with the Hamilton students.

The certainty of the rumor was made manifest
to Marjorie when, on Wednesday evening after dinner, she and Jerry heard a timid knock on their
door. Jerry, hastening to open the door, their caller
proved to be Anne Towne.

"Why, good evening, Miss Towne!" Jerry extended a hospitable hand. "So glad to see you.
We wondered what had become of you. We knew
you owed us a visit and were waiting for you to
pay it." Jerry ushered the wren-like freshman into
the room and offered her its most comfortable chair.

"I have been intending to call, but I—" Miss
Towne paused, looking rather confused. "You see
—I—didn't know but I might intrude. You girls
are so different from myself," she suddenly blurted
out, as though anxious to bare her diffident soul to
her dainty hostesses and have it over with. "I mean
different because you aren't poor and have lots of
friends and can entertain them and all that. I know
it is the custom at college for the upper class girls

to be kind to entering freshmen. I didn't care to presume on your kindness. I hope you understand me." She flushed painfully.

"Nonsense," scoffed Jerry sturdily. "We aren't a bit haughty. We want you to be our friend and hope to see you often. You mustn't think about such things. Just go along with your head held high. If people don't like you for your own merits, they are not worth cultivating."

"I believe you couldn't have been so very much afraid of Jeremiah's and my great dignity or you wouldn't have dared come and see us tonight." Marjorie smiled encouragement at the still embarrassed girl.

"Perhaps I wasn't really." Marjorie's winning smile communicated itself to the other girl. Her tired little face brightened wonderfully. "I am sure I won't be afraid ever again. I would love to call both of you my friends."

"Do so; do so." Jerry's instant response in a pompous tone made Miss Towne laugh. Marjorie thought her pretty when she laughed. Her teeth were unusually white and even, and her face broke into charming little lines of amusement.

"I will," she promised. "I came to you tonight for advice. You were all so kind to me the other day, I thought you wouldn't mind my asking you something. I have received an invitation to a picnic next Saturday to be given to the freshman class. Here it is."

Miss Towne opened a small handbag and drew from it a heavy white envelope. The faint odor of perfume still clung to it. Drawing from it a sheet of paper to match, she handed the latter to Marjorie. It read:

"DEAR MISS TOWNE:

"The Sans Soucians will be glad to see you at a picnic, to be given in honor of the freshman class next Saturday afternoon, the weather permitting, at Pine Crest. Please meet the other members of the class in front of Science Hall, at half-past one o'clock. The trip will be made by automobile and the Sans Soucians will entertain at luncheon.

"Yours cordially,
"DULCIANA VALE, Secy. Sans Soucians."

CHAPTER XI.

THE DIFFERENCE IN PICNIC PLANS.

MARJORIE studied the invitation in silence. Then she handed it to Jerry. The latter read it and said "Humph!" in a disgusted tone.

"I didn't know what I ought to do about it," broke in Miss Towne anxiously. "Who are the Sans Soucians? I've read quite a little of college sororities. I suppose they are a sorority. Would they be offended if I didn't go? I can't really spare the time. I do my own laundering on Saturday afternoon. The landlady allows me to use the kitchen. I don't mind telling you girls that. I would rather not give it as an excuse to the Sans Soucians, though. Perhaps I would not be missed if I didn't go. Do you think I would be? Are you girls members of the Sans Soucians?"

"Well, hardly!" Jerry spoke on the impulse of the moment. Miss Towne looked at her with increasing anxiety. Jerry's response was not indicative of flattery to the Sans Soucians.

"The Sans Soucians are a private club of eighteen

juniors," Marjorie quickly explained. "They live here at the Hall. They are all girls from very wealthy families and they entertain a good deal among themselves. They have taken an unusual interest in the freshmen since they came back to college. We heard that they intended to give a picnic in honor of the freshies. I believe I would try to go if I were you. It will be a good opportunity for you to meet the other members of your class. Besides, Pine Crest is such a beautiful spot. The afternoon in the fresh air will do you good."

Jerry gazed at Marjorie, a slight frown puckering her forehead. It was a fair-minded answer and just like Marjorie. Still, it went against her grain to help the Sans' cause along in the slightest degree.

"Have you met any of your classmates yet?" she asked abruptly. Without a little freshman support Jerry was not sanguine of Miss Towne's enjoyment of the picnic. The Sans' hospitality was not to be trusted.

"I know four girls a little who live several houses below me. They have the third floor of the house and do light house-keeping. They are very much pleased with the invitation. I wish they would ask me to go with them. I hate to go alone. I will accept, though, so long as you think it best." She turned to Marjorie with a kind of meek trust that touched the latter.

"Perhaps these other freshmen will ask you," was Marjorie's hopeful rejoinder. "If they shouldn't you will see them at the picnic and be with them anyway, perhaps. I know an even better plan. Suppose we get the rest of the girls, Jerry, and go over to Silverton Hall. We can introduce Miss Towne to the freshies there and she will be sure to have company at the picnic."

"All right, Marvelous Manager. I'll go and round them up." Jerry rose and promptly disappeared in search of her chums.

"I don't think I ought to go," demurred Muriel, when invited. "I have a hundred lines of French prose to translate. It's terribly hard, too."

"Translate it when you come back," suggested Jerry.

"I see myself doing it. It is half-past seven now. We'll be back here about ten minutes before the ten-thirty bell. That will give me a lot of time to translate a hundred lines. Now won't it?"

"Oh, come along. I'll see that you get back by nine-thirty, even if we have to start home ahead of the others," glibly promised Jerry.

"I'll see to it myself," declared Muriel. "I intend to be a stickler for duty this night. Go and get Ronny and Lucy while I do my hair over. It's all falling down. I will meet you down stairs."

Lucy and Ronny also raised weak objections on

the ground of unprepared recitations. Nevertheless they shut up their books with alacrity. Neither cared to be left out of a visit to Silverton Hall.

Presently the six girls were crossing the campus under the autumn stars. It was a soft October night and none of the Lookouts had donned hats or wraps. Walking between Marjorie and Ronny, Miss Towne began partly to understand how very delightful some girls could be. She had never had an intimate girl friend and she thought it remarkable that these self-possessed, beautifully dressed girls should be so ready to show her every kindness.

"You dear things!" was Robin Page's greeting as she fairly pranced into the living room at Silverton Hall not more than three minutes after her callers' arrival. "You certainly are unexpected but awfully welcome. Come up to my room this minute."

Robin smiled in friendly fashion at Miss Towne, although she had never met her. Immediately she had been introduced to the lonely freshman, and Marjorie had stated the object of their call, Robin said heartily:

"I will go and hunt up our freshies as soon as you are up in my room. Phil is there, of course. She rooms with me, you know. She swears she isn't going to that picnic. I don't know what the others think about it. Once get them together, it will be a good chance to find out."

Ushered into Robin's room, the Lookouts and their charge found Phyllis looking girlishly pretty in a flowered silk kimono. She received them in the pleasant, straightforward way they so greatly admired in her and proceeded to show an especial friendliness to Miss Towne.

Presently the murmur of voices outside announced that Robin had been successful in her quest. In fact she had found all seven of the freshmen in their rooms and had rushed them a la negligee to her own.

"Here we are," she breezily announced, "and not a freshie missing. I'll proceed to the great introduction act. Then, make yourselves at home."

As both groups of girls were bent on being friendly, a buzz of conversation soon arose. Under cover of it Robin said to Marjorie: "What do you think about the Sans' new stunt? You know just why they are doing it and so do all of us who fought out that basket-ball affair with them last year. Their motive isn't a worthy one. Still we really can't tell the freshies that. Phil understands matters. That's why she doesn't care to go. I know you want Miss Towne to go, or you would not have brought her over here tonight to get acquainted with our freshies. She will be safe from snubs with our girls. They are all fine. Too bad, but I don't trust the Sans even to do this stunt in a nice way. They will be sure to get haughty and hurt some freshie's feelings before their picnic is over."

"I have no faith in them, but it would be hardly fair not to give them the benefit of the doubt," re- turned Marjorie earnestly. "I wish Phil would go. It would be a good opportunity for the freshmen to see what a fine president they might have in her. She is so individual. I think she would be popular in her class in spite of the Sans' influence."

"So do I. You ask her. Maybe she will change her mind for you." Robin looked concernedly to where her cousin sat talking animatedly to Muriel and Miss Towne.

The latter, however, had already broached the sub- ject of the picnic to Phyllis.

"I am so glad to meet all you girls. Miss Dean suggested coming over on account of that picnic for the freshmen," Miss Towne had remarked inno- cently. "I had made up my mind not to go, but she thought I ought to and said if I met some other freshmen I would not have to go alone. I don't live on the campus so I haven't much opportunity of meeting other students."

"I see," nodded Phyllis. A swift tide of color had risen to her cheeks. From the instant she had set eyes on Marjorie Dean she had adored her. She now felt as though she had been lacking in true college spirit. If Marjorie thought Miss Towne should attend the picnic, undoubtedly she must think that the rest of the freshmen ought to do likewise.

"I will play especial escort to you at the picnic," she now laughingly offered. "I hadn't intended to go either, but I have changed my mind. Oh, Marjorie," she called across the room, "I'll take care of Miss Towne at the picnic."

"Will you, truly?" The eyes of the two girls met. A silent message was exchanged. "Then she will be sure to have a nice time," was what Marjorie put into words.

Robin and Marjorie also exchanged sly smiles. Each suspected that humble little Miss Towne was responsible for Phyllis's sudden change of mind. More, it was apparent that Phyllis had taken one of her sudden likings to the unassuming freshman.

Later, Robin found an opportunity to confide to Marjorie that she didn't know how it had happened, for Phil was terribly obstinate when once she had set her mind against a thing. Nor did Marjorie know until long afterward that she had been responsible for a decision on Phyllis's part which was the beginning of a warm friendship between Phyllis and Anna Towne.

Meanwhile the prospective hostesses of Saturday's outing were spending the evening in Leslie Cairns' room squabbling over their plans for the picnic. They could not agree on the refreshments, the amusements, or, in fact, anything pertaining to the affair. The truth of the matter was they were already tired of their beneficent project. They had never made a practice of unselfishly trying to please others, and the process bade fair to be too difficult for their infinitely small natures.

For once, during the wrangling that went on, Leslie Cairns honestly tried to keep her temper. The straw that broke the particular camel's back in her case, however, was an extended argument between Dulcie Vale and Natalie Weyman regarding the refreshments. These two, with Harriet Stephens, had been appointed to look after the luncheon. Harriet lazily expressed herself as indifferent to what the menu should be, provided it was fit to eat.

"Cut out this scrapping and get down to business, you two," finally ordered Leslie in her roughest tones. Followed an insulting rebuke from her that brought a flush to both the wranglers' cheeks. When thoroughly exasperated Leslie spared no one's feelings. "You decide on what to have *right now* and make a list of it. Trot it over to the Colonial early tomorrow morning. If you leave it until even tomorrow night they may refuse to handle it. Remember it will take time to pack a luncheon for one hundred and twenty-eight persons."

"Dulcie wants to serve a regular six-course dinner out in that neck of the woods," sputtered Natalie. "I am not in favor of such extravagance. It will cost us enough to have sandwiches, salads, relishes and sweets. Then there's coffee, chocolate, and imported ginger ale besides. I am not going to spend my whole month's allowance on a feed for those greenies."

"If we expect to make an impression on the freshies we ought to do things in good style," Dulcie hotly contested. "I don't care how much money it costs me. I have plenty of coin. The trouble with you Nat, is you're stingy. You buy everything expensive for yourself, but you are always broke when it comes to treating."

"I'll never forgive you for that, Dulice Vale," was Natalie's wrathful retort. "I think you are too——"

"That will be *all*," Leslie cut in sternly. "I said cut out the scrapping, didn't I? Either do as I say or get out of here. We can run the picnic minus either of you. Nat is right for once. Why should we spend a fortune on this affair?"

Knowing that Leslie would have no scruples about barring them both from further part in the picnic, they sullenly subsided. Dulcie freezingly accepted the list of eatables Natalie had made up and temporary peace was restored. Natalie bade Leslie a very cool goodnight a little later when the session broke up. She was hurt and angry over Leslie's brutal frankness. For an instant she wished she might be entirely free of Leslie's domineering sway. It was one of those moments when a faint stirring of a better nature made her long for harmony and peace. Her ignoble side was too greatly in the ascendency however to make her distaste for Leslie Cairns and her tyranny more than momentary.

CHAPTER XII.

A RECKLESS DRIVER.

"The Sans have certainly had one beautiful day for their picnic, but if they don't put in an appearance pretty soon they will be caught in a rain." Seated beside Marjorie and Lucy Warner in the big porch swing, Jerry squinted at the rapidly clouding sky.

While the day had been warm and moderately sunny, dark clouds had been looming up here and there in the sky since four o'clock. Scattered at first, they had gradually banked solidly in the west, obscuring the sunset and promising rain before nightfall.

"What time is it, Jeremiah?" asked Lucy. "I promised to meet Katherine here on the veranda at five-thirty. She left her handbag at Lillian's last night and we are going to walk over there before dinner."

"Why, Luciferous!" Jerry fixed Lucy with an amazed eye. "Can I believe that you and your

precious watch have parted company even for a
brief half hour!"

Lucy giggled. Her extreme fondness for the
wrist watch Ronny had given her was well known
to her chums.

"I broke the crystal," she confessed. "It
dropped from my hand the other night on the lavatory floor. I miss it terribly you had better believe.
It will be fixed tomorrow, thank goodness."

"Surprised at such carelessness. Ahem!" Jerry
teased. "If you want to know the time, it is twenty-
seven minutes past five. Your kindred spirit should
appear in three minutes."

"Here she comes now." Marjorie had spied
Katherine coming up the walk.

"Did you think I was going to be late?" Katherine called from the bottom step. "I had an awful
time looking up some data at the library. I just left
there and ran half the way here. It looks like rain,
but, if we walk fast, we can go over to Wenderblatt's and back before it starts. Want to go along,
Marjorie and Jerry?"

"I might as well. I've nothing else to do before
dinner. Come on, Jeremiah. A fast walk before
dinner will be a splendid appetizer." Marjorie rose
from the swing and brushed down her wrinkled
linen skirt.

"Don't need an appetizer. I'm famished now.

Lead me on. I may lose half a pound. That will be something attempted, something done, as our friend H. W. Longfellow sagely remarks in the 'Village Blacksmith.'"

Without further lingering the four girls left the veranda and started down the drive at a swift walk. The Wenderblatt's residence was not far from the campus, but the sky was growing more threatening.

"It begins to look as though we would have to run all the way back to the Hall or get a ducking," warned Jerry as they neared Lillian's home. "We can't stop to talk, girls. We had better wait for Katherine at the gate. If the whole gang of us goes up to the house we will lose time."

"Yes, I want to be back at the Hall for an early dinner. I must study like sixty this evening, for I won't have a minute tomorrow. Chapel in the morning, and I have promised to go over to Houghton House tomorrow afternoon with Leila. Then we are all going to Muriel's and Hortense's Sunday night spread. Sunday seems the shortest day in the week," Marjorie ended with a little regretful gesture.

"I'll be back directly." Coming to the high gate of the ornamental iron fence which inclosed the professor's property, Katherine clanged it hurriedly after her and sped up the walk to the house.

True to her word it was not more than ten minutes before she rejoined them, her handbag swinging from her arm.

Lillian was so sorry you wouldn't come up. She invited us all to dinner. I told her we simply must hurry back to the Hall. She——"

A sudden deep rumble of thunder drowned Katherine's speech. It was followed by a sharp blinding flash of lightning.

"We had better run for it," counseled Jerry. "There will be more thunder and lightning before the rain really starts. Don't let a little thing like thunder worry you, children."

By common consent the quartette broke into a gentle run. Soon they were on the highway and not more than a block from the campus wall. As they neared the east gate a terrific reverberating peal of thunder rent the air. So completely did it obliterate all other sound that none of the four heard the purr of a motor behind them, driven at excessive speed.

"Look out!" A sense of impending danger warning Jerry to turn her head, even in full flight, her voice rose in a sharp scream.

Her friends heard it dimly as the speeding car bore down upon them. Jerry made a wild dive out of harm's way, dragging Marjorie, who was nearest to her, with her. Lucy, who was on the outer edge of the road made a stumbling step backward.

Katherine——Through a mist of horror the three girls saw the machine catch her, flinging her off the road. They heard cries issue from the black and white roadster as it shot down the road.

"Katherine! Oh, do you suppose she is dead?" Already Lucy was kneeling on the ground beside the silent form in an agony of suspense. "She was almost in the middle of the road. I didn't have time to warn her. I didn't hear it until it ran her down." Lucy's face was white and set.

"Her heart's beating." Marjorie knelt at Katherine's other side, her hand inside Katherine's pongee blouse. "Better go over her for broken bones, Lucy." Marjorie was trembling violently though her voice was steady.

"It was Leslie Cairns who did that!" Jerry hotly accused. "I wonder if she'll have the decency to come back. She must know she ran some one down. I heard the girls in her car scream. I guess she turned in at the gate. Keep off the road, girls. Here come the rest of the picnickers. One accident is enough for today. She was speeding. That's why she was so far ahead of the others. I shall hail this first car and make 'em take Katherine up to the Hall."

Jerry did not need to hail the car. In the fading daylight the girl at the wheel, who happened to be

Margaret Wayne, brought her automobile to a stop almost even with the roadside group.

"What has hapened?" she called out sharply.

"Your friend Miss Cairns just ran down Miss Langly," returned Jerry grimly. "She isn't dead, but we don't know how badly she may be hurt. May we have the use of your car to take her to the Hall?"

"Certainly," came the response in frightened tones. Next instant the seven occupants of the car had piled out of it and gathered around the still unconscious girl.

A swift patter of raindrops struck the group, beating gently on Katherine's white, upturned face. Marjorie had now lifted her head to an easy position on her lap.

"Have any of you smelling salts?" she inquired calmly of the frightened circle, "or perhaps you have a water bottle with you."

"The luncheon things are in one of the cars away back. We have no water with us. Won't the rain help to revive her?" Margaret Wayne asked lamely.

"We shall not give it time to do that," Marjorie returned dryly. "If you will help us lift her we will get her into the car at once. It is only two or three minutes' drive to the Hall."

The others of the party being freshmen, they willingly sprang to Marjorie's assistance. Raised from the ground, Katherine opened her eyes and groaned a little.

"What—happened? Oh, I—remember. My back! It—hurts—so." She closed her eyes wearily.

Slender though she was, it became no easy matter to place her in the tonneau of the automobile. The credit of the undertaking went to Marjorie and Jerry, who exerted their young strength to the utmost for their injured friend. By this time a procession of automobiles containing the returning picnickers was drawn up along the road. The sound of excited voices from within these cars bade Marjorie lose no time.

"Will you please drive on before the others come up?" she entreated. "They know now that something has happened. We ought not to have a crowd around. I hope your passengers won't mind walking to the campus."

"Not a bit of it," assured two or three of the freshmen who had heard her remarks.

"Thank you." Marjorie flashed the group of girls one of her beautiful, kindly smiles which none of them forgot in a hurry.

Alarmed though she was by the accident, Margaret was half resentful of Marjorie's calm manner. Still she had no choice but to do as she was requested. She inwardly wished that Leslie had had the prudence to drive moderately. This affair was likely to make trouble for them all.

"Ready?" she interrogated, turning in the driver's seat to Marjorie.

An affirmative and she started her car for the Hall. Just at the gate they met the black and white roadster. Leslie was its sole occupant now.

"Hello!" she hailed. "Is that you, Margaret? What was the matter back there? Do you know?" Leslie leaned far out of her car in the gathering twilight.

"Your roadster hit Miss Langly. I don't know how it happened. She is in my car. Her friends are with her. You'd better go on down and tell the rest what has happened. They have stopped back there."

"What?" This time Leslie's pet interjection came involuntarily and with a tinge of fear. "I saw a bunch of girls, but I was sure I didn't hit any of them. See you at the Hall." Leslie started her car without further words.

"She has nerve!" muttered Jerry. "She thinks she is going to slide out of this easily. Well, she can't lay this outrage to anyone else. She had no business to be exceeding the speed limit. She never sounded a horn, either. Poor Kathie! I hope she isn't badly hurt."

"I—I—am all right, Jerry." Katherine had

heard. "The car just brushed me; hard—enough to throw me—on my back. That's all."

"That's all," repeated Lucy indignantly. Enough, I should say. Musn't talk much, Kathie. You'll be in your room and in bed right away."

"Glad of it. So—tired," mumbled Katharine, and closed her eyes again.

The injured girl was carried into the Hall just as a driving rain began to descend. Miss Remson promptly telephoned for her own physician and bustled about, an efficient first aid, until he arrived.

Established temporarily on the living room davenport, Katherine braced up wonderfully under the wise little manager's treatment. To her plea that she could walk upstairs to her room, if assisted by two of her friends, Miss Remson would not listen.

"Wait until the doctor comes, my dear," she insisted. "He will know what's best for you."

News of the accident having spread through the Hall, girls hurried from all parts of the house to the living room, where they were promptly headed off by Lucy, Marjorie and Jerry from intruding upon Katherine. Thus far neither the Sans nor the four freshmen who roomed at the Hall had put in an appearance.

The arrival of Doctor Thurston, a large, kindly man of about forty, was a relief to all concerned.

Very gently he lifted Katherine in his strong arms and carried her upstairs to her room.

"She has had a narrow escape," he told her anxious friends, a little later. "Her back is sprained. It is a wonder it was not broken. Two weeks in bed and she will be all right again. Students who drive their own cars should go slowly along the campus part of the road. There are always girls in plenty on foot. The one who ran her down must have had very poor policy not even to sound a horn."

CHAPTER XIII.

A PAINFUL INTERVIEW.

As a result of a private conference among the Lookouts that evening, a trained nurse arrived on Sunday afternoon to look after their injured friend. Ronny, with her usual magnificent generosity, wished to take the expenses for Katherine's care and treatment upon herself. To this her chums would not hear. "We all love Kathie," Muriel declared. "I think we ought to divide her expenses among us." Lucy Warner was particularly pleased with Muriel's proposal. She had earned an extra hundred dollars that summer by doing typing in the evenings. She felt, therefore, that she held the right to offer a portion of it in the cause of her particular friend.

"It seems too bad to go on having good times with poor Kathie so sick," deplored Marjorie, as she and Jerry softly closed the door of the latter's room after a brief visit to her following their return from Houghton House.

"I know it, but what good will it do us to cut out
recreation, so long as we can't spend the time with
her?" argued Jerry. "We know she is all right
and going to get well. It isn't as though she wasn't
expected to live. The nurse said a lot of the girls
had come to her door to inquire for her. She
wouldn't let any of 'em see her. I think the Sans
have been on the job. They are probably scared
for fear Kathie will make it hot for Leslie Cairns
when she is well again."

"She wouldn't." Marjorie shook her curly head.
"Neither would I, if I were in her place. It ought
to be a lesson to the Sans without any further fuss
about it. They are the only ones who drive faster
than they should."

"If Miss Cairns had run down a citizen of the
town of Hamilton then there would have been a
commotion. It is a very good thing for her that a
traffic officer wasn't around. He would have ar-
rested her, sure as fate. I wish one had been on the
scene," declared Jerry, with a trace of vindictive-
ness.

That the Sans were manifestly uneasy over the
accident was evidenced by their gathering in Leslie
Cairns' room that afternoon for a confab. Leslie
herself hid whatever trepidation she was feeling
under an air of cool bravado. She listened to all
that her companions had to say on the subject with-

out vouchsafing more than an occasional curt reply.

"Really, Les, you don't seem to understand that you may get into an awful mess over running down that beggardly dig!" Joan Myers at length exclaimed in sharp irritation. "Suppose the whole thing is put before President Matthews or the Board. We may all lose the privilege of having our cars at college. I read of a college out west the other day where that happened as the result of an accident to a student."

"Oh, forget it!" Leslie waved a derisive hand. "I shall fix things O. K. Don't make any mistake about that. I'll send this beggar a whopping old basket of fruit tomorrow and a handsome box of flowers. You girls had better part with a little change in the same cause. Anyway, I have pretty solid ground to stand on. Who is going to prove that I didn't sound a horn? It couldn't be heard above the thunder. If I drove fast, I had reason for it. Why should I drive my car at a crawl and be caught in the storm? Was there a cop around to say I was speeding? There was not. I certainly won't ever admit it. It was simply one of those unfortunate accidents. So sorry, I'm sure. What?" Leslie finished in a high, mocking treble.

It raised a laugh, as she intended it should. Her companions began to breathe more freely. Leslie could certainly be relied upon to clear herself.

Before evening of the following Monday Katherine's room resembled a combination fruit and flower market. Not only the Sans but her real friends and impersonal sympathizers also sent in their friendly tributes. Her condition much improved, she asked particularly to see Marjorie and Lucy Warner.

"Not more than fifteen minutes, please," said the nurse, as the two girls tip-toed into the sick room shortly before dinner.

"I wanted to see you so much." Katherine smiled a trifle wanly. "You were so good to me when first I was hurt. I remember the whole thing. I won't try to talk of that now. Later, when you can stay longer. There is something I wish you would do for me. Nurse read me the names of the cards on the flowers and fruit. The Sans sent a good deal of it. I—I—" a thread of color crept into Katherine's pale cheeks. "I don't want it. I can't bear it in the room. I understand them so well. I don't care to be harsh, but I would like you to take all of it except a basket of fruit and a few flowers and send it to the Hamilton Home for Old Folks. It is on Carpenter Street. It would please them so much. I can't eat one-tenth of the fruit before it spoils, and you girls don't want it, I know. If it is mostly all sent away, then no one can feel hurt, neither the Sans nor my real friends. The

Sans need not be afraid. I am not going to make Miss Cairns any trouble. She has asked twice to see me. I shall see her when I am a little stronger and tell her so."

"That is sweet in you, Kathie," Marjorie approved. She referred not only to Katherine's lenience of spirit toward Leslie Cairns, but to her proposed thoughtful disposal of the fruit and flowers. "I'll ask Leila to take your gifts to the old folks in her car tomorrow. I know she will be glad to be able to do something for you. I understand how you feel about—well—some things. I believe I'd feel the same if I were in your place."

"I wanted to be excused from my classes and be your nurse, Kathie," Lucy solemnly assured her chum, her green eyes full of devotion. "Ronny said 'no' that a trained nurse would be best. I miss you dreadfully. Let me come and see you every day, won't you?"

"Of course, you dear goose," Katherine assured, her blue eyes misting over with sudden tears. It was so wonderful to be loved and missed. "I shall not be in bed for two whole weeks. I can sit up a little now and I am so strong I shall be walking about the room by the last of this week. I am not used to being an invalid and I don't intend to get used to being one."

Naturally sturdy of constitution, the end of the

ensuing week found Katherine able to make little journeys about her room. It was not until the Friday following her accident that she felt equal to seeing Leslie Cairns. The nurse had informed her on Thursday that Miss Langly would be able to see her for a few minutes on Friday afternoon. Leslie accordingly cut her last afternoon recitation in order to call on Katherine before any of her friends should arrive on the scene.

"Good afternoon," she saluted without enthusiasm, as the nurse admitted her to the sick room. Her small dark eyes shrewdly appraised Katherine, who was lying on her couch bed clad in a dainty delft blue silk kimono.

"Good afternoon, Miss Cairns," Katherine returned. "Please take the arm chair. It is more comfortable than the others."

"Thank you. I can't stay long. I have been trying to see you for the last week; ever since your accident, in fact. Glad to see you better. I sent you some fruit and flowers. Tried to make you understand that I was anxious about you." Leslie paused. Her small stock of politeness was already threatening to desert her. She despised Katherine for her poverty. Now she disliked her even more because she had injured her.

"I thank you for the fruit and flowers. I asked the nurse to thank you for me when I received them.

COLLEGE SOPHOMORE   155

I have met with so many kindnesses since I—since
I was hurt." Katherine referred to the injury she
had received through Leslie's recklessness with
some hesitancy.

"You understand, don't you, that I wasn't really
to blame for your accident?" The question was put
to Katherine with brusque directness. I was driving a little faster than usual to escape the storm. I
was well within the speed limit. Remember that.
I fail to understand why you girls didn't hear my
horn. It sounded clearly, even above the storm."

"I did not hear it." Katherine fixed her clear
eyes squarely upon the other girl. "I heard Jerry
scream 'Look out!' and then the car struck me."

"Hm! Well, all I can say is you girls should not
have been strung across the road as you were," was
Leslie's bold criticism.

"We were walking only on the half of the road
used by cars coming toward us," was Katherine's
quietly defensive rejoinder. "But it doesn't matter, Miss Cairns. I do not intend to make any
trouble for you. I hope all excitement of the accident has died down before this."

"It will be dropped unless that crowd of girls you
go with keep stirring it up," retorted Leslie. "I
wish you would ask them to let it drop. Since you
are willing to, why shouldn't they be? I wasn't to
blame. Start an inquiry and the result will be we'll

not be allowed to keep our cars at college. That will hit some of your friends as well as myself and mine."

"I give you my word that I shall drop the matter. I know my friends have no desire to keep it active. I say this in their defense. I cannot allow you to misunderstand or belitle their principles."

Katherine spoke with marked stiffness. She could endure Leslie's supercilious manner toward herself. When it came to laying the fault at the door of her beloved friends—that was not to be borne.

"I'm not in the least interested in your friends. All I want them to do is to mind their own business about this accident. If you say they will, I look to you to keep your word. If you will accept a money settlement, say what you want and I will hand you a check for that amount." Leslie made this offer with cool insolence.

"Please don't!" Katherine was ready to cry with weakness and hurt pride. "I—won't you look upon the whole affair as though it had not happened? Money is the last thing to be thought of."

"Very well; since that is your way of looking at it." Leslie rose. She experienced a malicious satisfaction in having thus "taken a rise out of the beggar." Her point gained, she was anxious to be gone. "Hope you will soon be as well as ever. If you need anything, let me know. I must hurry along. I have a very important dinner engagement this evening. Goodbye."

She made a hasty exit, without offering her hand in farewell. Katherine lay back among her pillows with a long sigh of sheer relief. She felt that she could not have endured her caller two minutes longer without telling her frankly how utterly she detested her.

Marjorie and Jerry coming cheerily in upon her soon after classes, she confided to them the news of Leslie's call.

"The idea," sniffed Jerry. "Wish I had been here. I'd have told Miss Bully Cairns where she gets off at. How does she know but that President Matthews knows about it already? There were several freshies in her car. No doubt they were all her sort or they wouldn't have been with her. Look at the freshies in Miss Stephens' car. They were the first on the scene and were awfully sweet to us. What would hinder any one of them from 'stirring things up' if they disapproved of the way Miss Cairns acted? I mean the way she took her time about coming back after she ran Katherine down. She had better make the rounds of the college and tell everyone to keep quiet about it."

"She knows she is entirely in the wrong," said Marjorie sternly. Further, she has not told the truth. I am sure I would have heard a horn if she had sounded one. She was certainly exceeding the speed limit, and she did not keep her car to the proper side of the road. So long as Katherine wishes the matter dropped, her wish is law in the matter.

CHAPTER XIV.

A VOLUNTEER MESSENGER.

WHILE the news of Katherine's injury soon spread about the college, it was reported merely as one of those unintentional happenings for which no one was actually culpable. The owners of cherished cars were canny enough to realize that to capitalize the accident meant jeopardy to their privileges. All knew that a certain important college for girls had recently banned cars. None were anxious that Hamilton College should find cause to do likewise.

There was one person, however, upon whose action no one had reckoned. That particular person chanced to be Professor Wenderblatt. As a friend of his daughter's and his most brilliant pupil, the professor cherished a warm regard for Katherine. One of the freshmen in the car driven by Harriet Stephens chanced to be a friend of Lillian's. The latter received from her a fairly accurate account of the accident on the following Monday. Nor did the freshman fail to place the blame where it belonged.

Highly indignant, Lillian regaled her father with the news at dinner on Monday evening, declaring that she thought something ought to be done to make the Sans stop their reckless driving. Professor Wenderblatt, who was bound by no ties of school-girl honor, decided to have a private word on the subject with President Matthews. The fact that Katherine had just missed having her back broken was serious enough in his belief to warrant a reprimand from headquarters to the offenders.

Utterly unaware that she had a zealous, but an undesired defender, Katherine returned to her classes after a two weeks' absence apparently in good trim. With her re-appearance on the campus the Sans took heart again. Leslie had not been summoned to the president's office. Nothing had occurred to point to trouble from that direction.

The disastrous ending of the freshman picnic had dampened her ardor for electioneering for a few days. Gradually it returned. Aided by Lola Elster and Alida Burton, who were eager to please her, Leslie endeavored again by means of luncheons, dinners and treats to rally the freshmen to Elizabeth Walbert's banner. Certain wise freshmen, however, had discovered for themselves Phyllis Moore's many good qualities. They intended to nominate her and proceeded to root energetically for her. This contingent had not been pleased with the patronizing manner which the Sans had displayed towards them at the picnic. They were altogether too independent and honorable to barter their class vote for a mess of pottage.

"Freshie election this afternoon," announced Jerry, as she caught up with Marjorie on the steps of the Hall. "Saw you half way across the campus. You might as well have been ten miles away. I trilled but you didn't hear me. I'll bet that election will be a brisk and busy affair."

"I didn't hear you trill. I saw you just as I started up the walk. I hear Phil has quite strong support. It would be great if she'd win after all the fuss the Sans have made over Miss Walbert."

"She says she won't," was Jerry's disappointing reply. "She thinks over half the class will vote for Miss Walbert. If they do I shall be sore enough at them to stay away from the freshman frolic."

"There's to be a class meeting tomorrow afternoon to discuss that very frolic. Did you see the notice yesterday?"

"Yep. Nothing gets by me that I happen to see. I saw that," Jerry made humorous reply. "I suppose it is up to us to do the agreeable this year, also the decorating."

"Also the gallant escort act. Oh, my!" Marjorie exclaimed in sudden consternation. "Something important nearly got by me. I promised Miss

Humphrey this noon to give Lucy a message from her. Her secretary is sick and she needs someone for a few days. She is away behind in her letters. Goodbye. I'll see you later."

Marjorie promptly disappeared into the house in search of Lucy. Her quest proved fruitless. Lucy was not in her own room or with any of the other Lookouts. Katherine was also not at home, which pointed to the fact that the two had gone somewhere together.

"They're at Lillian's," guessed Marjorie. "I had better walk over to Hamilton Hall and tell Miss Humphrey I haven't seen Lucy," was her next thought. "She may be waiting for her."

It was not more than five minutes' walk across the campus to the Hall. Marjorie ran part of the way and bounded up the steps of the building, breathless and rosy.

"It was kind in you to take so much trouble, Miss Dean," Miss Humphrey said gratefully, as Marjorie explained Lucy's non-appearance.

"It was no trouble at all. I will surely see Miss Warner tonight. I wish there was something I could do to help you. I'm afraid I'd make a very poor secretary." Marjorie smiled at her own lack of secretarial ability.

"There is a service you can do for me. May I ask, have you anything particular to do before din-

ner? Something occurred today in the routine of
the business of the college which makes it necessary
for me to send a note to Doctor Matthews or else
go over to his home to see him at once. He has not
been at the Hall today, and I feel that I should not
let this matter go over until tomorrow without, at
least, sending word to him. I can't go myself. My
work will keep me here until after six. Then I have
a meeting on hand tonight. If you will take a note
for me to the Doctor, I shall be eternally grateful."

"I'd love to," Marjorie responded heartily.

"That is truly a weighty matter off my mind,"
smiled the registrar. Immediately she busied herself with the writing of the note to be intrusted to
Marjorie.

"There will be no answer," she said to Marjorie,
when, fifteen minutes later, she handed the letter to
the willing messenger. "If Doctor Matthews is not
in, leave it with a member of the family. Please
don't intrust it to the maid. If it should happen
that no one is at home, then you had better come
back with it to my office."

"Very well." Feeling quite at home with Miss
Humphrey, whom she had liked on sight, Marjorie
drew herself up and saluted. "That is the way I do
at home," she laughed. "My mother is Captain to
me and my father General. I'm First Lieutenant
Dean. I'll endeavor to carry out your order like a

good soldier." Wheeling about with military precision, Marjorie saluted again and left the office. The registrar watched her go with a smile. She reflected that she had never known so beautiful a girl as Marjorie to be so utterly unspoiled.

Doctor Matthews' residence was situated at the extreme western end of the campus. Although Marjorie had passed it many times, she had never before had occasion to go there. She had never met the president of Hamilton College personally, and since she had known of Miss Remson's grievance she had experienced a certain loss of respect for him. She was therefore indifferent as to whether she delivered the letter to him or to a member of the family.

As she mounted the steps to his home, which looked like a smaller edition of Wayland Hall, the front door opened and a young woman stepped out upon the veranda. She was a tall thin girl with pale blue eyes and straight heavy brown hair. Her features non-descript, her entire make-up was colorless rather than interesting. As the two girls passed each other on the veranda, the tall girl cast a sharp glance at Marjorie. A close observer would have characterized it as distinctly unfriendly. Marjorie was not even aware of it. Her mind was not on the stranger.

"Is Doctor Matthews at home?" she courteously inquired of the maid who answered her ring.

"Yes, Miss. Who shall I say wishes to see him. Have you an appointment with him?"

"No. I have a letter for him from Miss Humphrey, the registrar. She has requested me to deliver it personally."

"Please come in. I will tell the doctor." The maid disappeared into a room at the right of the colonial hall. Quickly returning, she said: "In there, Miss." She pointed to the door which she had left partially open.

The president was seated at a flat-topped mahogany desk. He rose as Marjorie entered and came forward to meet her.

"Good afternoon," he greeted, in the deep, pleasant voice which made his addresses a delight to the ear. "Norah tells me you have a note for me from Miss Humphrey."

"Good afternoon," Marjorie returned. "Here is the note. Miss Humphrey said there would be no answer." She half turned as though to depart.

"Just a moment." The doctor was regarding her with keen but friendly eyes. "You are not of the clerical force at Hamilton Hall. Let me think. You are a sophomore, are you not?" He asked the question triumphantly, smiling as he spoke.

"Yes; I am a sophomore." Marjorie's brown eyes held polite amazement.

"I am very proud of my memory for faces," Doctor Matthews continued. "I rarely forget a face, though I do not always remember names. You were one of the freshman ushers at Commencement last June. Now you have come into sophomore estate. How do you like it?"

"Better than being a freshman." It was Marjorie's turn to smile. "I am so much better acquainted with Hamilton College now. I am sure there isn't another college in the world half so fine." She blossomed into involuntary enthusiasm. "Mr. Brooke Hamilton must have been a wonderful man. He planned everything here so nobly."

"He was, indeed, a man of noble character and true spirituality. I would rather be president of Hamilton College than any other college I have ever visited or been connected with. I revere the memory of Brooke Hamilton. It is unfortunate we know so little of him. His great-niece, Miss Susanna Hamilton, lives at Hamilton Arms. She is the last of the Hamilton family. Unfortunately for the college, she became incensed at the churlish behavior toward her of a member of the Board whose estate adjoined hers. This was many years ago. She had been on the verge of turning over to the college a great deal of interesting data regard-

ing Brooke Hamilton which was private family his-
tory. Doctor Burns, then president of Hamilton,
was to write the biography of the lovable founder
of our college. After the falling-out with the Board
member she refused to give up the data. Since then
she has ignored the college. Brooke Hamilton's
biography yet remains to be written."

"A case of the innocent having to suffer with the
guilty," Marjorie said, her eyes very bright. She
was privately exultant to have learned this bit of
news of the Hamiltons. She had heard that the
last of the Hamiltons, a woman, lived at Hamilton
Arms. Leila had told her a little concerning the
present owner of the Hamilton estate.

After a few further remarks on the subject of
Hamilton College, she gracefully took her leave.
As she stepped from the hall to the veranda, she
encountered the same young woman she had met
on her way into the house. This time the girl was
seated in one of the porch rockers. Her eyes, as
they fixed themselves on Marjorie, looked more
unfriendly than ever. Marjorie caught the hostile
import of this second prolonged stare.

"What a hateful face that girl had," she thought,
as she continued down the walk. "I don't recall
ever having seen *her* before. I'd certainly have
remembered that face. Perhaps she's a relative of
Doctor Matthews. She seems to be quite at home."

Returned to Wayland Hall, Marjorie's first act was to go to Lucy's room to give her Miss Humphrey's message. This time she found Lucy in but alone.

"Where's Ronny?" she inquired, after she had explained to Lucy the registrar's present difficulty, "I haven't seen her except at meals for two days."

"She's out with Leila and Vera waiting for the election returns. They are anxious to find out if Phil won."

"Hope she did," was Marjorie's fervent wish. "You can never guess in a thousand years to whom I was talking this afternoon."

"I'm a poor guesser. You'd better tell me," Lucy said in her concise fashion.

"All right, I will. It was President Matthews." Lucy's greenish eyes turning themselves on her in astonishment, Marjorie laughed, then went on to relate the circumstances.

Lucy listened with the profound interest of a wise young owl. "What do you think of him?" she asked reflectively, when Marjorie had finished. "Does he seem the kind of man that would do a person an injustice? I'm thinking of Miss Remson now."

"I thought of her, too, while I was in his office," Marjorie responded. "No; he doesn't appear to be anything but broad-minded and just. Still, we mustn't forget that his name was signed to that letter."

"Did you see his secretary?" Lucy quizzed. "She is over at his house some of the time. He is usually at Hamilton Hall until one o'clock in the afternoon, then he goes home. I understand he transacts a good deal of college business at his home office."

"I didn't see anyone but the maid who answered the door and the president. Oh, I'll take that back. I saw a girl coming out of the house as I was going up the steps. When I came out I saw her again. She was sitting on the veranda. She had *such* a disagreeable expression. I noticed it particularly the second time I saw her."

"Describe her," Lucy tersely commanded.

Marjorie complied, giving a fairly good description of the stranger.

"That girl——" Lucy paused impressively, "is the president's secretary."

"Really?" Marjorie's brown eyes opened to their widest extent.

"Yes; really. I told Miss Remson the morning we were in her office that I intended to find out all I could about Doctor Matthews' secretary. I have not found out anything much about her except that she is not a student. But I have seen her. Kathie knows her by sight. She pointed her out to me one afternoon. We passed her on the campus. She was

going toward Doctor Matthews' house. I did not
like her looks. I feel that she was at the bottom of
Miss Remson's trouble and it would not surprise
me to learn that she is in with the Sans. Unfortunately I have no way of proving it. I believe it,
just the same."

"There was something queer about that whole
affair," Marjorie agreed. "You remember Helen
said that, if the Sans were insolent and supercilious
when they came back to the Hall, it would mean
they had had information beforehand and were sure
of their ground. Well, they were very much like
that. They acted as though they owned the Hall.

"I noticed that, for I watched them particularly.
I think Miss Sayres, that's the secretary's name,
is the one who helped them. I hope some day to be
able to prove it."

CHAPTER XV.

THE RENDEZVOUS.

THE noisy entrance into the room of Muriel, Jerry, Leila, Vera and Ronny, with the disappointing news that Phyllis had lost the freshman presidency by only nine votes, broke up the confidential session.

"We went to our room first but you were not to be seen. Thought you'd be here. Last I saw of you you had started on a hunt for Lucy. Isn't it a shame about the election? To think that Walbert snip won!" Jerry elevated her nose in utter disapproval. "Won't the Sans crow? They will blow her off to dinners and spreads for a week to come. I hope she gets an awful case of indigestion."

"How very cruel you are, Jeremiah." Nevertheless, Ronny laughed with the others. Jerry's hopes for the downfall of her enemies were usually energetic and sweeping.

"I can be a lot more cruel than that," she boasted. "It made me tired to hear those sillies had elected that girl to the class presidency. Glad I'm not a

freshie. They will rue it before the year is up.
Phil's supporters are as mad as hops."

Many of the upper-class girls shared Jerry's opinion. The Sans' open championship of Elizabeth
Walbert had excited unfavorable comment on the
campus. While the upper-class students aimed to
be helpful elder sisters to the freshmen, college eti-
quette forbade a too-marked interest in freshman
affairs. The Sans had over-reached themselves and
were bound to come in for adverse criticism in college circles where tradition was still respected.

The Sans, however, were oblivious to everything
save the fact that they had gained their point. Leslie Cairns was radiant over the victory and gave an
elaborate dinner that evening at the Colonial in
honor of Elizabeth. Besides the Sans, Alida Burton and Lola Elster, twenty-two freshmen were
invited. She engaged the restaurant for the evening and spared no pains and expense to make the
dinner what she termed "a howler."

Following on the heels of her triumph strode
calamity. The mail next morning brought her a
letter which lashed her into a furious rage. It was
a terse summons to appear at Doctor Matthews'
office at eleven o'clock that morning. More, the
four lines comprising it had been penned, not typed.
Her instant surmise was that the summons had to
do with the recent accident of Katherine Langly.

She could think of no other reason for it, unless—
Leslie turned pale. There was another reason, but
she preferred not to give it mind room. She boldly
decided that she would ignore the letter that morning. She would receive a second summons. It
would be easy enough to assert that she had not
received a first. This would give her time to see a
certain person and perhaps gain an inkling of what
was in the wind.

An interview with the "certain person" yielded
nothing. That person was unable to throw light
upon the reason for the summons. Two days
elapsed, then Leslie received a second communication too austere to be disregarded. She went to the
president's office in considerable trepidation and
emerged from it an hour later, her heavy features
set in anger. Undertaking to assume her usual non-
chalant pose, she had been brought with alarming
suddenness to a wholesome respect for Doctor Matthews' dignity. She had also received a lecture on
reckless driving which she was not likely to forget.

"While it seems unfair to deprive students who
are careful drivers of the privilege of using their
automobiles at college, simply because careless
young women like you will not conform to the traffic
conditions, it will come to that." Doctor Matthews
was a study in cold severity as he made this threatening statement. "I shall take drastic measures if

another accident occurs as a result of speeding or reckless driving on the part of a student. I have been informed, Miss Cairns, that you are in the habit of exceeding the speed limit. It is a particularly dangerous proceeding on the highways adjacent to the college on account of the number of students who make a practice of walking. Referring to the accident to Miss Langly. What restitution could you have made if her back had been permanently injured? There is nothing more pitiful than a helpless invalid. Remember that and see that you are not the one to cause lifelong unhappiness or death by an act of sheer lawlessness. Let this be the last offense of this kind on your part."

Thus the president concluded his arraignment. Leslie left Hamilton Hall with but one flaming purpose. She would be even with the person or persons who had reported her to the president. Suspicion instantly pointed out "that Sanford crowd." She gave Katherine clearance of it, strange to say. She preferred to lay the blame at either the door of Marjorie or Jerry. Yet she had dark suspicions of Leila and Vera. Then there were the freshmen who had been in Harriet Stephens' car. Harriet had told her that they were in sympathy with Katherine's crowd. Whoever was to blame would suffer for it. On that point she was determined.

Shortly after her return to Wayland Hall, she resolved to cut her classes that day. Leslie received a telephone call. It was not unexpected. She had notified the maid that she would be in her room in case she should be called on the 'phone. Her sullen features cleared a trifle as she listened to the voice at the other end of the wire.

"All right," she said in guarded tones. The students had already begun to drop in from the last recitations of the morning. "Nine o'clock sharp. I'll walk. I'm not going to take chances of attracting attention. Yes, I know where you mean. It's not far from Baretti's. Don't fail me. Good-bye."

On her way to her room she encountered Natalie. "Come with me," she said shortly.

"Where were you this morning?" Natalie asked. "Professor Futelle was awfully fussed about absentees. Eight girls cut French today."

"Where was I? I was in bad, I'll say. What? Well, I guess. I got a second summons this A. M. I couldn't side-step it. His high and mightiness had the whole story of the accident from some tattle-tale. He wouldn't give me a chance to say a word hardly. One more break in the speeding line and our cars go home for good. He certainly laid down the law to me. I've a mind to tell you something else." Leslie paused before the door of her room, hand on the knob.

"What is it? You know I never tell tales, Les."
Natalie eyed the other girl reproachfully. "That's
more than you can say of your other pals."

"You are right about that, Nat," Leslie conceded.
She motioned Natalie into the room and closed the
door. "Laura says she knows who told Doctor
Matthews. I'm to meet her tonight. Keep that
dark. I don't want a person besides you to know
it. I'm to meet her behind that clump of lilac
bushes the other side of Baretti's. You know;
where that old house was torn down."

Natalie nodded. She was inwardly jubilant at
having thus been given Leslie's confidence. It was
quite like old times. "Have you any idea who
told?" she questioned, trying to hide her gratification under an air of calm interest.

"No. I'm positive it wasn't Langly. She gave
me her word that she would drop the whole thing.
A goody-goody dig like her would not break it. I'll
tell you as soon as I come back. Come here at ten.
I shall not be later than ten-fifteen. I intend to put
up a 'Busy' sign tonight so as to keep the girls out
of here before I start. They know better than to
try to get by it, too."

At precisely twenty minutes to nine that evening
Leslie took the "Busy" placard from her door and
locking it proceeded to the rendezvous. She had
put on a long dark motor coat and a black velour

sports hat. The instant she had left the Hall's premises behind her she pulled the hat low over her face and broke into a run. An expert tennis player, she was swift and nimble of foot. Only once she paused, stepping behind a thicket of rhododendron bushes until a party of girls returning from town passed by. Once off the campus, she kept to the darker side of the road and was soon at the designated spot.

Her brisk run had brought her to the meeting place ahead of time. It was five minutes before the faint sound of a footfall among the fallen leaves rewarded her small stock of patience. Leslie's hand sought the pocket of her coat. A tiny stream of white light outlined the figure now very close to her. Instantly she snapped off the light with a soft ejaculation of satisfaction.

"You should not have turned that light on me," objected the other dark figure rather pettishly. "We might be seen from the road."

"Not a soul passing," Leslie assured. "I was not going to take chances of hailing the wrong party."

"Please remember that I have to be even more careful than you. No one must ever be allowed to suspect that we know each other." Laura Sayres spoke with cool precision.

"Is that what you came all the way here to tell

me?" Leslie gave a short laugh. It announced that she was on the verge of being unpleasant.

"Of course it isn't." Laura prudently retreated from her lofty stand. While she enjoyed grumbling, she was too cowardly at heart to venture to do more. "I couldn't say a word over the 'phone today. I will tell you now and quickly for I have a long walk home and the road is quite lonely in places."

"Sorry I couldn't bring my car, but I didn't dare," carelessly apologized Leslie. She divined that Laura was somewhat peeved because she had not.

"Oh, it doesn't matter. Now I don't know just how much this information will be worth to you—" Miss Sayres paused. "I can only—"

"Give it to me and I'll do the square thing by you." Leslie frowned in the darkness.

"Oh, I don't mean in money," weakly defended Miss Sayres. "I mean that it's circumstantial. You must form your own opinion from what I tell you."

"I understand." Leslie quite understood that despite the secretary's protest she was not above being mercenary. "Go ahead."

"Last Tuesday afternoon about five o'clock I was just starting for home from Doctor Matthews' house, when who should come marching up the walk but Miss Dean," related Laura. "I wondered what brought her there. As soon as the maid let her in I turned and went back. I had made up my mind to wait around until she came out. I have a key to the front door now. One day when college first opened the doctor sent me over to the house for some papers he needed. No one was at home and I had to go back to Hamilton Hall without them. He had a key made for me right after that. You see I occupy a position of trust. No wonder I have to be careful."

"I see; but what about Miss Dean?" Leslie promptly switched the secretary back to her original subject.

"I am coming to that. I decided after I got as far as the veranda to let myself into the house. I supposed Miss Dean had come to see the doctor. The minute I stepped inside I heard voices. The door of the office was open just a little. I did not dare stand in the hall so I slipped into the living room. It is directly opposite the office. I couldn't understand a word Miss Dean said, but I heard the doctor say he was incensed at the behavior of someone, and that they would have to come before the Board. Then he said that if someone, I couldn't find out who, refused to do something or other, she would have to leave college. It remained for him to write her.

"I heard Miss Dean say very plainly: 'It is a case of the innocent having to suffer with the guilty.' They talked a little more, but both lowered their voices. I heard the doctor's chair turn and knew he was going to get up from it. I made the quickest move I ever made and slid out the door. I had left it a little open. Sure enough, in a minute or two Miss Dean came out of the house and went away."

"I think that's pretty good proof against the foxy little wretch." Leslie's voice was thick with wrath. She was still smarting from the morning's humiliation. "I wish I could tell you how I hate that little sneak. I'll get back at her, believe me."

"I certainly would, if I were you. Just to be on the safe side I went into the house and stopped at the office door. I said, If you have nothing more for me to do I will go now, Doctor Matthews. I thought perhaps he would ask me to write the letter he had spoken of. Not he. He said: 'No, thank you, Miss Sayres. You need not have waited.' So I had no excuse to stay."

"That's another proof. The letter he sent me was penned. You have picked the culprit, all right enough. I have an idea I know how to deal with her." Leslie threatened in an excess of spite. "One thing more and then we must beat it. Do you believe that Remson affair will ever leak out? I shiver every time I think of it. That was a bold stroke."

"It doesn't worry me. I know enough about Miss Remson to know she will keep far away from Doctor Matthews after the letter she received from him. The one he received from her, after she had been over to see him, made him think she had had a heart-to-heart talk with you girls and you'd all promised to do differently. He wouldn't interfere after that. Unless they should happen to meet, which isn't likely, matters will stay as they are. I destroyed the letter supposed to be from Miss Remson. The doctor told me to file it, but if he ever asked for it I would pretend not to be able to find it. He wouldn't remember what she wrote. While I am his secretary I can manage the affair. As time passes it will be forgotten. Doctor Matthews would not mention it if he happened to meet Miss Remson. That's not his way."

"Glad to hear it. It lifts a weight from my mind. I've only one more year at Hamilton after this. My father expects me to be graduated with honor. He would never forgive me if I were to be expelled from Hamilton at this late date." Leslie was moved out of her usual indifferent pose. Fear of exposure gripped her hard at times.

"Better let this Miss Dean alone," was Laura's succinct advise. "I hear she is very popular on the campus. She looks independent enough to take up for herself. Be careful she doesn't turn the tables on you as she did last spring."

"Not this time. She won't like my methods, but she won't be able to prove that they are mine. In fact she won't know where to place the blame."

CHAPTER XVI.

FAIR PLAY AND NO FAVORS.

PHYLLIS MOORE accepted her defeat with the easy grace which was hers. Her freshman supporters were not so ready to give in. They gave up the ghost with marked displeasure. Forty-five members of the class had voted for her. They had shown open and hearty disapproval of Elizabeth Walbert. The other three officers were more to their liking, but the Sans' electioneering had left a rift in the freshman lute which promised plenty of discord later on. Though every member of the class had attended the picnic as a matter of courtesy, the finer element had been privately weary of the affair before the afternoon was over. The Sans' efforts to mould the freshmen to their views merely resulted in amalgamating stray groups to one solid formation. A fact they were presently to discover.

The election of officers had occurred much later than was the rule. The excitement attendant upon it had hardly died out before the freshman frolic

loomed large on their horizon. With the sophomore class almost entirely free from snobbish influ-
ences, the dance promised to be an occasion of undiluted enjoyment. The humbler freshmen off the
campus were the first to receive invitations from
the sophs. Those sophs who still clung to the Sans
were only a handful. The freshies of Elizabeth
Walbert's faction found that the majority of them
would be without special escort unless the juniors
or seniors came to their rescue.

Rallied to duty by Alida Burton and Lola Elster,
the Sans magnanimously stepped into the breach.
They, in turn, brought certain of their junior and
senior allies to the aid of the escortless. It was a
sore point, however, among a number of freshmen
who had voted for Miss Walbert that the sophomores had passed them by for mere off-the -campus
students. It served as a quiet lesson by which a
a few of them afterward profited.

Eager to regain her lost laurels, Natalie Weyman
was insistent that Lola and Alida should ask the
entertainment committee to give another Beauty
contest.

"What do you take me for?" was Lola's derisive
reply when Natalie asked her for the third time to
try to bring the contest about. "I'd just as soon
ask Prexy Matthews to dye his hair pink as to ask
those snippies to give a Beauty parade. Kiss

yourself goodbye, Nat. You didn't win it last year. Nuff said."

Whereupon Natalie took pains to confide to anyone who would listen to her that she thought Lola Elster the rudest, slangiest person she had ever had the misfortune to meet.

Marjorie could not recall a festivity for which she had worked hard beforehand and enjoyed more than the preparation for the freshman hop. Going to the woods to gather the spicy, fragrant pine boughs and gorgeous armfuls of autumn leaves and scarlet mountain ash berries for decorations was purest pleasure. No less did she revel in the hours spent in beautifying the gymnasium in honor of the baby class. Everyone concerned in the labor was so good-natured and jolly that an atmosphere of harmony permeated the big room and hovered over it on the night of the frolic.

Even the Sans appeared to imbibe a little of that genial atmosphere and behaved at the frolic with less arrogance than was their wont when appearing socially. Leslie Cairns alone of them flatly refused to be present. She wheedled Joan Myers into escorting Elizabeth Walbert to the dance and remained in her room in a magnificent fit of sulks. She was too greatly inflamed against Marjorie to endure going where she would be in close touch with her for an evening. She therefore amused

herself that evening in planning the cherished move
she intended to make against Marjorie.

"Perhaps I ought not say it, but I had a good
deal better time tonight than at the frolic last year,"
Muriel confided to her chums between yawns. Dis-
cipline being lax they had gathered in Ronny's and
Lucy's room after the dance for a cup of hot chocolate and sweet crackers.

"I know I had," emphasized Marjorie. "Everyone seemed to go in for a good time tonight."

"The Sans unbent a little, didn't they?" commented Jerry. "That was because their boss stayed
away. Those girls might become civilized in time
without Leslie Cairns on the job."

"They were a little more gracious," agreed
Ronny. "I don't know how the rest of you feel
about it. I am glad the frolic is over. I am tired.
We have been stirred up ever since we came back to
college. First over Miss Remson's trouble. Next
came the Sans' move to grab all the freshmen.
Then Kathie's accident, and after that the commotion over the freshie election. We were all keyed
up to quite a pitch over that on account of Phil.
Now the dance is over. What next? Nothing, I
fondly hope. I am going to lead the student life,
provided I am allowed to do it."

"You forget basket ball," reminded Muriel.

"I am going to try to forget it," retorted Ronny

so wearily that her tone elicited a chorus of giggles.
"I don't play the game, thank my stars!"

"I shall, if I have a chance," Muriel asserted.
"How about you, Marjorie?"

"I am going to try for a place on the team this
year," Marjorie announced in a purposeful manner.
"I hope we get a fair try-out. I really want to play.
I like Professor Leonard's appearance. Helen had
quite a long talk with him the other day. He is a
seasoned basket ball player. He played center on a
western college team the whole four years of his
college course. He is going to arrange for a series
of try-outs to be held next week. He thinks each
class ought to have its own team. The seniors
never play, though."

"Since those are his sentiments, they sound as if
he were strictly on the square," approved Jerry. "I
mean, he is a real basket-ball enthusiast. The real
ones won't stand for unfairness."

"Miss Reid will be a cipher in b. b. plans this
year and I am good and glad of it," exulted Muriel.
"Professor Leonard looks to me like a person who
wouldn't show favoritism. He certainly has lots of
the right kind of energy."

Muriel's opinion of the young professor of physical culture proved correct. On Monday following
the freshman dance, a notice appeared on the official
bulletin board stating that on Tuesday, Wednesday,

Thursday and Friday afternoon of that week basket-ball try-outs for freshman, sophomore, junior and senior teams, respectively, would be held at four-thirty o'clock in the gymnasium. It bore the pertinent signature: "James Leonard, Director Athletics and Gymnasium."

Freshmen and sophomores hailed it with delight. The juniors were not so enthusiastic, though it was noised about that there would be a junior team composed of Sans, if they could manage to make it. The seniors from the height of their dignity smiled tolerantly but refused to commit themselves.

Determined to be in touch with the game from the very beginning, Muriel, Jerry and Marjorie attended the freshman try-out. Ronny begged off on account of a chemical experiment she was anxious to make. Lucy declared, that, if she attended the sophomore try-out on Tuesday she considered that a sufficiency of basket ball.

Under the expert and impartial direction of Professor Leonard, the freshman try-out was conducted with a snap and precision which left nothing to be desired in the minds of those students who had yearned for fair play. It brought confusion to a certain clique of freshmen, headed by Elizabeth Walbert, who had reckoned on some of their particular friends carrying off the honors and being appointed to the team. The despatch with which the aspirants were made up into squads and tried out against each other was a joy to witness. The energetic director weeded out the defective players in short order. His searching eyes missed not a movement, clever or bungling. The five girls finally picked to play on the official freshman team were a survival of the fittest. Among them was Phyllis Moore. Further, she was given the position of center and roundly complimented by the director for what he termed her "whirlwind" playing. This triumph pleased boyish Phyllis far more than winning the class presidency could have done. Barbara Severn, the Baltimore freshie, who Marjorie had looked out for on her arrival at Hamilton, won the position of right guard, and was also praised for her work.

Once the team was chosen the director put them through fifteen minutes of snappy play. Their fast and nimble work elicited rousing cheers from the large audience of students who had dropped in to witness the try-out.

"Isn't it great that both Phil and Barbara won?" bubbled Robin Page. Half a dozen Silverton Hall girls had joined Marjorie's group after the try-out, preparatory to giving the successful aspirants a special ovation as soon as they should leave the floor. "Phil and Barbara are awfully chummy, so they'll be pleased to the skies."

"I think they are a great combination," returned
Jerry. "They are our catches. We hooked them
when we went freshie fishing. I like the way they
look after Anna Towne, too. She is lucky to have
them for pals."

"Phil is very fond of her, you know," smiled
Robin, "and Barbara is a dear. She is a real South-
ern aristocrat. She has the gentlest, kindest ways
and the sweetest voice! She and Phil are the really
great hopes of the freshman class, I think."

"You know what the Bible says about the little
leaven leavening the whole lump." Jerry spoke
with sudden seriousness. "Maybe Phil and Barbara
will turn out to be the particular kind of leaven the
freshies need. I suppose they wouldn't feel esp-
cially complimented at being classed as a 'lump,'
but then what they don't hear will never hurt them,"
she added, her serious face breaking into its irresist-
ible little grin.

"I only hope we do as well tomorrow as Phil and
Barbara," Muriel said irrelevently, her brown eyes
fixed in some trepidation on the alert director.
"That man's eyes seem to be everywhere at once.
Nothing gets by him."

"We will have to hustle if we expect recognition
from him, I know that. There are some fine players among the sophs, too. You know how well that
team chosen after the fuss with Miss Reid could

play. I think Robin is a better player than I," Marjorie turned to Robin with a smile.

"No, siree! I have heard marvelous reports of your playing," differed Robin with energy.

"You have a bitter disappointment ahead of you tomorrow then," retorted Marjorie. "You'll probably see me relegated to the scrub, sub or dub class."

"I prophesy all three of you modest violets will make the team. The real exhibition will be on Thursday afternoon. The strenuous Sans and the dictatorial director; or, what's the use without Miss Reid? They will learn a few points of the game before he gets through with them. I wouldn't miss that try-out for a good deal." Jerry was deriving an impish satisfaction from the prospect of the Sans' encounter to come with Professor Leonard.

The next afternoon brought a large and interested audience to the gymnasium. Robin Page had many well wishers in all three of the upper classes. Leila and Vera also headed a goodly company who were anxious to see Marjorie and Muriel make the team. The Sans came in a body to cheer Lola Elster and Alida Burton on to victory. They had attended the freshman try-out and seen a team selected which contained not one of their allies. They had also learned that Professor Leonard was not to be deceived for an instant. Only the fairest kind of fair play would be acceptable to him. Leslie

Cairns was confident that Lola Elster would make the sophomore team. Of the skill of her junior chums as players she was openly doubtful. She rudely hooted at their avowed intention to enter the lists.

"You girls are punk players, one and all. Why make simpletons of yourselves tomorrow?" she inquired of Joan and Natalie. "You need at least a month's drill to put you in trim. Proffy Smarty Alec will chase you off the floor."

"You're so hateful, Les," bitterly complained Joan. "We stand as good a chance as can be at the junior try-out. I happen to know that we Sans are almost the only juniors who are going to try for the team. Some of us will be picked. He's a fine coach. He will soon put our team in good form."

"Go to it and be happy," Leslie laughed. "You will so enjoy being ragged every three minutes by that conceited tyrant. I am not going to throw cold water on your fond hopes, but don't cry if he can't see you as a junior team."

CHAPTER XVII.

"GENERAL" CAIRNS TO THE RESCUE.

THE series of try-outs, plus the directorship of
Professor Leonard, caused basket ball interest to
soar to exceptional heights. The sophomore try-
outs brought even a larger number of students to
the scene than did the freshman test. About thirty-
five sophs essayed to make the team. None of the
aspirants could be classed as poor players, and it
took the approving director a trifle longer than at
the previous try-out to pick the team.

Muriel was among the first two fives to be called
to the floor. Always to be depended upon in by-
gone high school days, she had not fallen off as a
player. During the fifteen minutes of brisk play,
she was conspicuous by reason of her clever work
with the ball. Watching her eagerly, Marjorie
could only hope to do as well when her turn came
to play.

At Sanford High School she had often been rated
by enthusiastic fans as the star player of the school.

She had formerly loved the game and played it with all her might. Now the old delightful fascination for it thrilled her anew. She forgot everything save the fact that she was once more to tussle for the ball. Robin Page had been called to the opposing five. From the moment Professor Leonard put the ball in play at center she and Marjorie amply demonstrated their right to be classed as stars. Applause was not slow in coming from the interested spectators. The sophs raised their voices in cries of "Robin Page! Marjorie Dean!—Who are they? They're all right! Some players! Rah, rah, rah!" and similar calls of noisy appreciation. Even Professor Leonard smiled at the racket that ensued when Marjorie made a clever throw to basket after spiritedly dodging her opponents.

When finally the try-out ended and the official soph team was named, it consisted of Robin, Muriel, Marjorie, Grace Dearborn and Marie Peyton. To Marjorie fell the honor of center and a more delighted, astonished girl than she would have been hard to find.

"You deserve center," Robin delightedly wrung her hand. You are a better player than I and I don't mind a bit. Oh, Marjorie! Think what fun we shall have whipping all the other teams. We have a wonderful five!"

This was the consensus of opinion. Knowing

fans were already predicting easy victories for the sophomore team that season. The moment the winning five had been announced Lola Elster disappeared. Her mortification at having failed to make the team would not permit her to remain and meet the Sans. She knew Leslie Cairns would be disappointed, and, consequently, in a bad humor. Her own state of chagrin was such that a word from Leslie would have brought on a quarrel. Lola prudently decided to vanish until the keen edge of Leslie's displeasure should have worn itself off.

The fast playing they had witnesssed that afternoon went far to dampen the Sans' ardor to try for the junior team. That evening they held a consultation in Joan's room on the subject. In the end, however, they could not resist the desire to make themselves prominent. They agreed to play their best, and, if chosen, to hire a coach and practice assiduously. Leslie was present at the discussion and brimming with derision. "You had better keep off the floor," was her rough advice. "You'll make a worse showing than Lola did and she was hopeless."

Spurred by Leslie's jibes the Sans resolved to put forth every effort at their try-out to make a decent showing. Other than themselves there were not more than half a dozen aspirants. Thus their chances were good. Having closely watched the director's methods at two try-outs they knew what would be expected of them. They had also learned a number of things about basket ball that they had not known before. Whether they could apply this knowledge to their own playing on such short notice was a question.

When the fateful junior try-out was over, Professor Leonard was of the private opinion that he had made a mistake in attempting to carry basket ball beyond the sophomore year. Nevertheless he selected a team from junior material, such as it was, and proceeded to tersely address them. Joan Myers, Natalie Weyman and Harriet Stephens represented the Sans. The other two players chosen were a Miss Hale and a small sprightly junior, Nina Merrill.

"You young women are all sadly out of practice. You can play a fair game if you go to work and spend some time on the floor. You are away behind the freshmen and sophomores. You would be white-washed by either team if you met them now. Your playing is too slow. Learn to move fast. That is essential in basket ball. On a man's team, the moment a player begins to show a slowing down he is dropped. Quick work; that is the beauty of this game. Come here regularly for practice and I will help you."

The frank opinion of the director, delivered in

impersonal kindness, the Sans found hard to swallow. Self-willed and self-centered, they bore honest criticism very badly. Neither were they appreciative of his offer to aid them in their practice.

"I think it is fine in Professor Leonard to offer to help us," ventured Nina Merrill to Joan Myers as the director walked away. The team had been standing in a group during the short address.

"Really, I hadn't thought about it." Joan's tones were chilling. Nina was a nobody in her estimation and must be treated as such.

"You must be most unappreciative." Stung by the snub she had received, Nina spoke straight from her heart. Then she turned and walked away.

"Why, the idea!" An angry flush overspread Joan's face. To be treated to a dose of her own medicine did not set well.

Just then Leslie Cairns joined them and Joan forgot her outraged feelings.

"Come along," ordered Leslie. "Get your togs changed in a hurry. I am going to blow you three girls to eats at the Ivy. Beat it out of the dressing room without saying where you're going. I want to talk to you three and I am not strong for entertaining the gang. You did better than I thought you would. What was Leonard haranguing you about?"

"He raked us down for being out of practice.

Said he would coach us if we'd come regularly to the gym." Natalie made a contemptuous gesture.

"Tell him to fly away," shrugged Leslie. "You don't need his coaching. I have a better plan. Let's be moving."

The quartette walked away without a word of farewell to Ruth Hale, who had been standing near them. She was also beneath their notice.

"You had a lot to say about *our* punk playing before the try-out, Les. What do you think of Lola? She certainly didn't distinguish herself." Natalie could not conceal her satisfaction at Lola's failure.

"Don't mention it." Leslie's heavy brows met. "I was sore enough at the little dummy to shake her. She let the other five put it all over her. I haven't seen her since she flivvered and I don't want to."

"She never could play basket ball," was Natalie's lofty assertion.

"She didn't show any signs of it yesterday," Leslie grimly agreed. "I'll meet you girls at the garage," she directed with a brusque change of subject. "I am going over there for my car. It's good way to lose the gang. They won't look for us there."

"What do you think of Les?" inquired Joan with raised brows as the two girls entered the dressing room. "Before Lola flivvered she was simply insufferable. Today she is positively affable. She's down on Lola. That's one reason."

"I wish she'd stay down on her," responded Natalie with fervor. "Les and I have never been as good pals since Lola Elster entered Hamilton."

"Now listen to me, Nat. Leslie likes you just as well as she ever did." Joan broke forth with some impatience. "She runs around with Lola and Bess Walbert, I know, and makes a fuss over them. She is perfectly aware that it makes you sore. She does it to be tantalizing. Les likes to keep something going all the time. It is a wonder to me that she hasn't been expelled from college for some of the tricks she has put over. What you must do is to pay no attention to her when she is aggravating. Don't quarrel with her. She enjoys that. Simply behave as though you couldn't see her at all. It will cure her. I'd rather see her chummy with you than Lola or Bess, either. Bess Walbert can't tell the truth to save her neck, and Lola is a selfish kid who thinks of no one but herself."

"That's all true, Joan," Natalie said with unusual meekness. "I will really try to treat Les as you suggest."

It was not necessary that evening to treat Leslie as Joan had advised. She was amiability itself. After ordering dinner, composed of the most expen-

sive items on the menu, she rested her elbows on
the table and announced: "I am going to hire a
coach for you three girls. I have the address of an
all-around sportsman who will teach you a few
plays that no one can get by."

"But, Les, we can't do much with only three to
play," objected Joan. "You don't want those two
sticks of juniors at our private practice do you?"

"Not so you could notice them. You won't have
to play a trio. The coach will make four and——"
Leslie paused. "I shall make a fifth. I need the
exercise. The coach needs the money. Besides, I
propose to hire a hall."

Joan and Natalie tittered at this last. Leslie
smiled in her loose-lipped fashion.

"I met this man at the beach last summer. He
was coaching a private track team. He knows
every trick in the sports category. He told me
there were lots of ways of fussing one's opponents
in basket ball besides treating them roughly. He
said he had a regular line of what he called 'soft
talk' that he had used with splendid effect. He
gave me his address and said if ever I needed his
services to write him. I had told him enough about
the game here so he understood me. I understand
him, too. This is my idea," she continued, leaning
far forward and lowering her voice.

For ten minutes she talked on, her listeners paying strict and respectful attention.

"It's a great plan," admiringly approved Joan when Leslie had finished. "It will take cleverness and nerve, though."

"I doubt if I can do it," deprecated Harriet.

"Certainly you can do it. After you work a week or two with this coach and learn his methods you will be O. K. You will have to give three afternoons a week to it; maybe more. I'll drive to Hamilton and hire that hall tomorrow. I'll wire the coach before we go back to the campus tonight. He's in New York and I can have him here by Saturday."

"It's going to cost oodles of money. Why are you so bent on doing it, Les?" Joan asked curiously.

"I won't be kept out of things." Leslie turned almost fiercely upon her questioner. "I loathe that nippy Robina Page and I hate Marjorie Dean and her crowd. They can play basket ball, I'll admit. I'll show them they are not the only stars. You girls have got to take a game away from them. You are not to play them for a while. You are to whip the freshies first. They are a handful, too. Later, you are to beat the sophs. With the help of Ramsey, this coach, you can do it, and I know it."

CHAPTER XVIII.

"THE SOFT TALK."

THE senior try-out did not take place on Friday. No aspirants appeared at the gymnasium. The seniors were not ambitious to shine as basket-ball stars. The freshmen went to work at once to perfect their playing under the willing guidance of Professor Leonard. The soph team was not quite so zealous, but put in at least two afternoons a week at practice. This team was the pride of the active director's heart. He assured them more than once that they could meet a team of professional men players and acquit themselves with credit. If he wondered why the junior five did not take advantage of his offer, he made no comment. While he took a deep interest in basket ball, he left all the arrangements of the games to the senior sports committee, preferring to allow them to do the managing.

Owing to the delay in forming the teams, no games were scheduled to be played until after

Thanksgiving. Directly college routine was resumed after that holiday the freshmen challenged the sophomores to meet them on the eighth of December. The sophs graciously accepted the challenge and beat the freshies after one of the hardest fought contests that had ever taken place at Hamilton. The score stood 24-22 in favor of the sophs when the game ended, and the tumult which ensued could be heard half way across the campus. The freshmen had fought so gallantly they came in for almost as much acclamation as the winners.

Ready to give the defeated team an opportunity to square itself, the sophs challenged the freshmen to meet them on the following Saturday. The unexpected illness of Phyllis Moore, who contracted a severe cold on the eve of the game, resulted in a postponement. The freshmen team did not wish to play without Phyllis, though they announced themselves ready to do so by appointing a sub to her position. The sophs, however, would not hear to this. Thus the postponement was satisfactory to all concerned.

The junior team, in the meantime, were keeping strictly in the background. Secretly the coach, Milton Ramsey, had been established in a hotel in the town of Hamilton and was busily engaged with Leslie's team. Never had Joan, Harriet and Natalie had to work so hard. Not only must they practice in secret. Leslie decreed that they would have to practice in the gymnasium with the other two chosen members of the team in order to keep up appearances. She was a hard taskmaster, but she kept her companions in good humor by expensive presents and treats. Further, she assured them that once they had beaten the sophs they could drop basket ball for the rest of the year.

The rest of the Sans were not blind to the fact that the four girls were deep in some private scheme of their own. Coolly informed by Leslie to mind their own affairs and they would live longer and wear better, they gossiped about the situation among themselves and let it go at that. The majority of them were not doing well in their subjects and they were constrained to turn their attention for a time to the more serious side of college.

Christmas came, with its dearly coveted home holidays, and the Lookouts gladly laid down their books for the bliss of being re-united with their home folks and beloved friends. This time Lucy Warner spent Christmas at home, taking Katherine with her. A four weeks' illness of Miss Humphrey's secretary had given Lucy the position of substitute. This unexpected stretch of work had furnished her the means with which to spend Christmas with her mother. The registrar privately remarked to President Matthews that Lucy was the most able secretary she had ever employed.

For a week following the Christmas vacation, spreads and jollifications were the order in the campus houses. As Jerry pensively observed, after a feast in Leila's room, the world seemed principally made of fruit cakes, preserves and five-pound boxes of chocolates.

"I'm always crazy to go home at Christmas, yet it is pretty nice to be back here again," she remarked to Marjorie one evening soon after their return to Hamilton, as she sealed and addressed a long letter to her mother.

"I am so homesick the first two or three days after I come back that nothing seems right," Marjorie said rather soberly. "College soon swallows that up, though. I think about General and Captain just as often, but it doesn't hurt so much. Goodness knows we have enough to busy us here. My subjects are so difficult this term. Then there's basket ball. The freshmen are clamoring now for a game. Our team will re-issue that challenge soon, I know."

"What do those junior basket-ball artists think they are going to do, I wonder?" Jerry tilted her nose in disdain. "I hear they are practicing quite regularly in the gym. They simply ignore Professor Leonard. I mean the three Sans. Miss

Hale and Miss Merrill are awfully cross about it.
They have to play with the team, and it seems Leslie
Cairns is coaching it, or trying to."

"I heard she was. I didn't know she could play.
Funny the juniors don't challenge either the freshies or us."

"They wouldn't win from either team." Jerry
shook a prophetic head. "The Sans seem to have
settled down to minding their own affairs since
Kathie was hurt. I guess that subdued them a
little. They slid out of that scrape easily. Hope
they practice minding their own business for the
rest of the year. Ronny says she is amazed that
they can do so."

Three days later the sophomore team re-issued
their challenge. Sent to the freshmen on Monday,
the game took place on the Saturday after. Another
battle was waged and the score at the close of the
game was 28-26 in favor of the sophs. It seemed
that the freshmen could not surmount the fatal two
points. Deeply disappointed, they bore the defeat
with the greatest good nature. They were too fond
of the victors to show spleen. Nothing daunted,
they challenged the sophs to meet them again two
weeks from that Saturday.

The next Monday a surprise awaited them.
They received a challenge from the junior team to
play them on the Saturday of that week. Though

not enthusiastic over the honor, they accepted. Nor could they be blamed for being privately confident that they would win the game. It stood to reason that if they could so nearly tie their score with the sophs, the juniors would not be difficult to vanquish.

When Saturday rolled around and the game was called, they took the floor, quietly confident of victory. It seemed as though the entire student body had turned out to witness the game. There had been plenty of comment on the campus at Leslie Cairns' sudden whim of acting as coach. Curiosity as to what kind of showing the juniors would make as a result of her efforts at coaching had brought many girls to the scene.

Before the game began the freshman team were somewhat puzzled at the extreme affability of the three Sans' members of the opposing team. The trio met them as they emerged from the dressing room and hailed them as though they had been long lost friends. The impression of this unexpected cordiality had not died out of the five freshmen's minds when the toss-up was made. As the game proceeded they became dimly aware that this fulsome show of affability was being continued. Pitted against the junior team, as they were, it was most annoying. Nor did the three Sans play the game in silence. Whenever they came into close contact with one or more of the freshmen, they had something to say. It was not more than a hasty sentence or two uttered in a peculiarly soft tone. The effect, however, was disconcerting. Soon it became maddening. Involuntarily the one addressed strained the ear to catch the import. A sudden exclamation or ejaculation would have passed unnoticed. This purposely continued flow of soft remark drew the attention of the hearer just enough to interfere with both speed and initiative.

Not until the first half of the game had been played did it dawn fully upon the freshmen that they were being subjected to an interference as unfair as any bodily move to hamper would have been. Further, the three girls were doing it very cleverly. It was not hampering their playing in the least. Ruth Hale and Nina Merrill were playing with honest vim and in silence. Their sturdy work was equal to that of any of the opposing team save Phyllis. She was as brilliant a player as her cousin, Robin Page. Being, however, of a nervous, high-strung temperament, the three Sans' tactics had effected her most of all. As a consequence, she missed the basket two different times. Besides that, she grew disheartened with the thought that she was playing badly and missed opportunities at the ball that would never have ordinarily slipped by her.

The end of the first half of the game found the

score 12-8 in favor of the juniors. The instant it was over Phyllis, who captured her team, gathered them into one of the several small rooms off the gymnasium.

"Girls," she said, in low intense tones, her blue eyes flashing, "you understand what those three Sans are trying hard to do. Miss Hale and Miss Merrill are innocent. We can complain to the sports committee and stop the game, but I'd rather not. Basket ball rules ban striking, tripping and such malicious interferences. They don't ban talking. These cheats know it. They annoyed me, because I wasn't expecting any such trick. I never played worse. We are four points behind. It's principally my fault, too. All we can do with dignity to ourselves is to try not to notice their ragging during the second half."

"Queer kind of ragging," sputtered Janet Baird. "If they'd say mean things we'd know better how to take them. Miss Weyman said right in my ear, last half, 'You freshies certainly play a fast game. How do you do it?' Her voice was as sweet as could be. It got on my nerves. Only for a second or so, but long enough to take my attention from the ball. That was her object."

The other members of the team had similar instances to relate. The ten minutes' rest between halves was turned into an indignation meeting.

When the recall whistle blew, the incensed five took
the floor in anything but the collected, impersonal
mood the game demanded.

The three Sans had spent their intermission talking to Leslie. She was in high good humor over the
success of her scheme. "You have them going.
Don't let up on them a minute. See that they don't
make up those four points. Hale and Merrill are
playing finely."

"They don't suspect a thing, either," declared
Natalie. "I am afraid those freshies will set up a
squeal to the sports committee if we win."

"If? You must win. No ifs about it," decreed
Leslie. "What can they say? You haven't broken
the rules of the game. If they make a kick about
it they put themselves in the sorehead class."

Thus encouraged by their leader, the elated trio
returned to the floor primed for more mischief.
Advised by Leslie, they kept quiet during the first
five minutes. Expecting to be again assailed by the
irritating murmurs, the freshmen met with a welcome silence on the part of their tormentors. It
lasted just long enough for the ragging to be
doubly irritating when it began afresh. Now on the
defensive, the freshman five steeled themselves to
endure it with stoicism. Nevertheless, it was a
strain and put them at a subtle disadvantage. They
managed to make up two of the points they had

lost. Fate then entered the lists against them. Janet Baird made the serious mistake of throwing the ball into the wrong basket. This elicited vociferous cheering from junior fans and spurred their team on to the fastest playing they had done since the beginning of the game. Needless to say they dropped their unfair tactics at the last and fought with fierce energy to pile up their score. The freshmen also picked up on the closing few minutes, but the game ended 24-20 in favor of the juniors.

The losing team made straight for their dressing room, there to relieve their pent-up feelings. Very soon afterward they were visited by the sophomore team. They had attended the game in a body and had not been slow to see that things were all wrong.

"Don't feel down-hearted about it," sympathized Marjorie, as Janet Baird began bewailing her unlucky mistake of baskets. "We know how things were. So do lots of others. If the juniors should challenge you to another game, don't accept the challenge. We sophs hope they will challenge us. We think they will and try the same tactics with us. Then we are going to teach them one good lesson. After that we shall ignore them as a team."

CHAPTER XIX.

A CLAIM ON FRIENDSHIP.

AFTER the sophomore five had heard a detailed account from Phyllis of what had occurred on the floor, they were more determined than ever on punishing the three offenders. The awkward hitch in their plans was the fact that Miss Hale and Miss Merrill, though players on the team, could not be included in their team mates' misdoings.

"Some one ought to tell those two girls how matters stand," was Ronny's energetic opinion. "They must have been very dense not to see and hear for themselves. If they noticed nothing was wrong during the game, they must surely have heard things since. It's no secret on the campus. Talk about a good illustration in psychology! It was a deliberate attempt at retarding action by a malicious irritating of the mind. I think I ought to cite it in psychology class."

Several days after the game Nina Merrill went privately to Phyllis and frankly asked her a number of questions. Receiving blunt answers which tallied with a rumor she had heard, she laid the matter before Ruth Hale and both girls resigned from the junior team. This put the remaining trio in a position they did not relish. The senior sports committee having received the resignations of the two indignant juniors accepted them without question. They appointed Dulcie Vale and Eleanor Ray, both substitute players, to fill the vacancies. As the Sans had been almost the only juniors to try for the team, the committee had little choice in the matter. Their appointment brought elation to their team mates and Leslie Cairns. "Ramsey will soon put them in good trim," she exulted. "Don't wait for those sulky freshies to challenge you. After the girls have had a week's practice, challenge the sophs and set the date two weeks away. That will give Dulcie and Nell plenty of time to learn the ropes."

The Saturday following the disastrous game between freshmen and juniors saw the freshmen actually tie their score with the sophs. According to fans it was "one beautiful game" and the freshies left the floor vastly inspired after their defeat of the previous week. Meanwhile the sophomores calmly awaited the junior challenge. They were better pleased to have the junior team composed entirely of Sans. They would have a quintette of the same stripe with which to deal.

Before the challenge came, however, the St. Valentine masquerade, the yearly junior dance, given on February fourteenth, claimed attention. It was, perhaps, the most enjoyed of any Hamilton festivity. What girl can resist the lure of a bal masque? The socially inclined students often went to great pains and expense in the way of costumes. Three prizes were always offered; one for the funniest, one for the prettiest, and one for the most generally pleasing costume.

"I don't know what to wear to the masquerade," Marjorie declared rather dolefully. The Five Travelers were holding a meeting in hers and Jerry's room. "I'm in despair."

"Go as a French doll," suggested Ronny. "I have a pale blue net frock made over flesh-colored taffeta. It will be sweet for you. Shorten the skirt and it will make a stunning French doll costume. I have heelless blue dancing slippers to match."

"You're an angel. Isn't she, Jeremiah?" Marjorie became all animation. "What are you going to wear, oh, generous fairy god-mother?"

"My butterfly costume. The one I danced in at the Sanford campfire."

"What are you going to mask as, Jeremiah," curiously inquired Lucy. "Every time I see you I forget to ask you."

"I am going as an infant," giggled Jerry. "I

shall wear a white lawn frock, down to my heels, and one of those engaging baby bonnets. I shall carry a rattle and a nursing bottle and wail occasionally to let folks know I am around."

"I don't want to dress up, but I suppose I'll have to," grumbled Lucy. "I'll go as a school girl, I guess. I can wear a checked gingham dress I have and a white apron, by shortening them. White stockings and white tennis shoes will go well with it. I'll wear my hair down my back in two braids."

"I shan't tell you what my costume's going to be. Only you will never know me on that night." Muriel made this annoucement with a tantalizing smile.

"I would know you anywhere," contradicted Jerry. "I'll bet you a dinner at Baretti's that I'll walk up to you after the grand march and say 'Hello, Muriel.' "

"I'll bet you you don't," was Muriel's confident reply.

"This dance has put a large crimp in basket ball," Ronny suddenly observed. "It seems to be at a standstill. Vera said today that she heard the juniors had challenged you sophs."

"Not yet," returned Marjorie. "Robin heard the same thing. She mentioned it to me after chemistry today. Maybe we are due to get a challenge tomorrow. If we do we will not take it up until after the dance. We don't care to be bothered with it now. Do we, Muriel?"

"No, sir. After the masquerade is over we'll then turn our undivided attention to laying the juniors up for the winter. That may be the last game of the year, unless the freshies yearn for another. I am tired of playing, to tell you the truth. I don't intend to play next year."

"Nor I," Marjorie said. "I like the good old game, but it takes up so much of one's spare time. I shall go in for long walks for exercise. I have never yet prowled around this part of the world as much as I pleased."

"I see where I grow thin and sylph-like," beamed Jerry. "*I* shall accompany you on those prowls."

"I think I'll join the united prowlers' association, too," laughed Ronny. "I'd love to have a chance to prowl about Hamilton Arms, wouldn't you? I walked past there the other afternoon. They say that old house is simply filled with antiques. They also say that Miss Susanna Hamilton won't permit a student to set foot on the lawn. And all because she fell out with a member of the Board. He must have done something very serious."

"It is too bad she has shut herself away from everyone," Marjorie mused. "She is probably unhappy. Leila says she looks like a little old robin. Her hair isn't very gray and she is quite energetic.

She has a rose garden and digs in it a lot. Just to think. She could tell us the most *interesting* things about Brooke Hamilton and we don't know her and never will."

"Sad but true," agreed Jerry without sadness.

During the short time that lay between them and the masquerade, the Lookouts spent their free hours in arranging their costumes. Ronny had to mend a broken place in one of her butterfly wings. Marjorie, Lucy and Jerry had to turn needlewomen. While Marjorie and Lucy had to shorten the skirts of their costumes, Jerry busied herself in laboriously finishing the infant dress she had been working on for over two weeks. "I'll never go back to infancy again, after the masquerade, believe me," she disgustedly declared. "Let me tell you, this sweet little baby gown is fearfully and wonderfully made. I know, for I took every stitch in it."

The day before the dance the sophomore team received the junior challenge to play them on the twenty-seventh of February. Purposely to keep their unworthy opponents on the anxious seat they did not immediately answer the notice sent them. "Let them wait until after the dance," Robin Page said scornfully. "If we had not determined to teach them a lesson, we would turn down their challenge and state our reason in good plain English."

The evening of the St. Valentine masquerade was

always a gala one on the campus. Dinner was
served promptly at five-thirty. By seven o'clock, if
the weather permitted, masked figures in twos,
threes and groups might be seen parading the
campus. Eight o'clock saw the begining of the
grand march. Unmasking took place at half-past
nine. Then the dance continued merrily until midnight.

Hurrying from Science Hall after her last recitation of the afternoon, Marjorie crossed the campus
at a swift run. She was anxious to be early at the
lavatory for a shower before the girls began to
arrive there in numbers. Coming hastily into the
hall she glanced at the bulletin board. In the rack
above it, lettered with each resident's name, was
mail for her. She gave a gurgle of pleasure as she
saw that the topmost of two letters was in her mother's hand. The other was not post-marked, which
indicated that it had come from someone at the college. She did not recognize the writing.

Saving her mother's letter to read later, she tore
open the other envelope as she went upstairs. On
the landing beside a hall window she stopped and
drew forth the contents. Her bright face clouded
a trifle as she perused the note.

"DEAR MISS DEAN: it read:

"It is too bad to trouble you when I know you
are getting ready for the masquerade, but could

you come over to my boarding house for a few minutes this evening at about half-past seven? I am in great trouble and need your advice. I would ask you to come earlier but this will be the best time for me. We moved this week to the house two doors below the one I used to live in, so stop at 852 instead of going on to 856. If you can find it in your heart to come to me now I shall be deeply grateful. I am in sore need of a friend. Please do not mention this to anyone.

        "Yours sincerely,

              "ANNA TOWNE."

CHAPTER XX.

MARJORIE swallowed an inconvenient lump that rose in her throat. She would go to Miss Towne, but it meant a total up-setting of her plans. As she could not guess the freshman's trouble she could not gauge her time. She might have to be gone for some time, although the note read "a few minutes." It was too bad. She felt a half desire to cry with disappointment. If she went at once she could get it over with and not miss the dance. But, no; the note specified half-past seven as the hour.

Presently she rallied from her downcast mood and took sturdy hope. Perhaps, after all, she would not be detained long. She was sure Anna had done nothing wrong. It was more likely a financial difficulty which confronted her. That would not be so hard to adjust. Jerry would have to know. She decided that the other three Lookouts were entitled to know also. She might have to call on them for help in Anna's case. They were here close friends

and fit to be trusted with a confidence. She claimed
the right to use her own judgment in the matter.

"What a shame!" was Jerry's disgruntled reception of the news. "I think it is selfish in her. Why
couldn't she have waited until tomorrow? It is
probably a financial difficulty. She isn't the kind of
girl to break rules."

"A member of her family may have died and she
hasn't the money to go home. It must be realy serious," Marjorie soberly contended. "I ought to go
and I will. There is no snow on the ground. I
can dress before I go and wear high overshoes and
my fur coat and cap. Then, if I am not kept there
long, I can hustle to the gym and be there before
the unmasking."

Better pleased with this arrangement, Marjorie
hastily gathered up towels and toilet accessories and
trotted off to the lavatory, leaving Jerry to frown-
ingly re-read the note. Jerry did not like it at all.
She wondered why Miss Towne could not have
come to Wayland Hall instead of putting her chum
to the extra trouble of seeking her.

Dinner was eaten post haste that night by the
excited participants in the masquerade. Preparations having been the order so long beforehand, it
did. not take the maskers long after dinner to get
into their costumes. They were eager to go outdoors and parade the campus, the night being pleas-

antly snappy with an overhead studding of count-less stars.

Fearless in the matter of going out alone after dark where an errand called her, Marjorie did not mind the rather lonely walk after leaving the campus. In order to escape parties of maskers on the campus she wore her own mask and therefore escaped special notice. Without it she would have been challenged by every party of masks she met. This was a favorite custom on this night. Fre-quently a member of the faculty was caught in crossing the stretch of ground and gleefully inter-viewed.

Coming to the row of houses, in one of which Miss Towne resided, Marjorie kept a sharp look-out for the number. The house where she had formerly lived stood about the middle of the block. Finally she came to 852, which she found by means of a small pocket flashlight which she usually car-ried at night. The arc light was too far up the street to be of use to her in this.

Pausing at the bottom step of the dingy wooden veranda, Marjorie surveyed the house with a feel-ing of depression. The two windows on the left were without blinds and dark. There was a faint light in the hall and in the room on the right. The two windows of this room had shades. One was drawn down completely; the other was raised about eight inches above the sill.

"What a cheerless place," she murmured half aloud. "It is worse than the other house. I suppose the landlady hasn't got settled yet."

Mechanically she reached out and took hold of the old-style door bell. It did not respond at first. Using more force, it emitted a faint eerie tinkle. "It sounds positively weird," was Marjorie's thought. She smiled to herself as she rang it again. "I hope I shall never have to live in a boarding house like this. I am lucky to have love and a beautiful home and really every good thing."

The faint sound of footsteps from within falling upon her expectant ear, Marjorie straightened up and waited. A hand turned the knob. The door opened about ten inches.

"Good evening. Come in." Addressed in a muffled voice, Marjorie caught sight of a tall, black-robed figure. Before she could reply to the muttered salutation, she felt herself seized by the arms and drawn into the house with a jerk. Simultaneous with the harsh grasp of a pair of strong hands the light in the hall was turned out.

"Oh!" She gave one sharp little scream and exerting her young strength flung off the prisoning hands. "Keep your hands off me," she ordered bravely.

Just then the door leading from the hall into the right hand room opened. The light from several tall candles shone dimly into the hall. She saw that she was surrounded by half a dozen dominoed masks.

"Bring in the prisoner," grated a harsh voice from within the room. Despite Marjorie's command of hands off, she was given a sudden shove forward which sent her·roughly through the doorway and into the larger apartment.

Sureness of foot saved her from stumbling. Strange to say, she had now lost all fear of the company of masked figures in whose midst she stood. It had begun to enforce itself upon her that she had been hoaxed into visiting an empty house by those who had taken advantage of the masquerade to carry out their plan without undue notice to themselves. She was now certain that she was being hazed by students. She knew of only one group of Hamilton girls who would be bold enough to deliberately defy the strictest rule of Hamilton College.

The masked company were attired in black dominos; all save one who appeared to be a kind of sinister master of ceremonies. This one wore a domino of bright scarlet silk and a leering false face mask that was hideous in the extreme. The flickering flame of the candles added to the grim and horrifying effect. A girl of timid inclinations would have been sadly frightened. Marjorie was made of sterner stuff. She had experienced, briefly, actual terror when she felt herself seized and drawn into the house. She had now recovered from that and was righteously angry. She determined to assume contemptuous indifference, for the time being, preferring to allow her captors to play their hand first.

"Prisoner, you are now before the stern tribunal of the Scarlet Mask," announced the red dominoed figure in the same harsh guttural tones. "You have been guilty of many crimes and are to be punished for these tonight. If you obey my mandate you will escape with your wretched life. Disobey and nothing can save you. You are now to be put to the question by one who knows your treacherous heart. You will remove your outer wrappings and stand forth. Question." The red mask made an imperious gesture. A domino on the left stepped forward as though to lay hands on Marjorie.

"I shall not remove my coat, cap or overshoes." Marjorie's ringing accents cut sharply on the cold air of the unfurnished, unheated room. "If one of you undertakes to lay a hand on me you will be sorry; not only now but hereafter. I defy you to do it."

Standing almost in the center of the circle of

dominos, Marjorie cast contemptuous eyes about
the circle of maskers. She fully intended to defend
herself if further molested. She was one against
many, but she could at least fight her way to the
window, tear aside the shade and pound lustily upon
it, raising her voice for help. She was certain she
was in the hands of the Sans. She knew they would
not court exposure. They had reckoned on completely intimidating her.

A peculiar silence followed Marjorie's spirited defiance. It was as though the high tribunal were in
doubt as to what they had best do next. With one
accord their slits of eyes were turned on their
leader. The domino who had been ordered to lay
hold of the prisoner shied off perceptibly.

"Bring forth the charges against the prisoner."
The distinguished scarlet mask suddenly changed
tune. While the hideous face within the close-
fitting hood glared fiendishly at Marjorie, the real
face behind it wore an expression of baffled anger.
The unruly prisoner seemed in possession of an
inner force that forbade molestation. Then, too,
she was unafraid and all ready to make a lively
commotion.

A domino on the outer edge of the group came
forward with a roll of foolscap, tied with a black
silk cord. The cord impressively untied, amid dead

silence, and the paper unrolled, the reading of Marjorie's crimes was begun.

"Prisoner, you are accused of untruthfulness, treachery and malicious interference in the affairs of others. It is not our purpose to detail to you the occasion of these crimes. These occasions are known to the high tribunal and have been proven against you."

"It is my purpose to demand proof," interrupted Marjorie with open sarcasm. "I am not untruthful, malicious or treacherous. I do not propose to allow anyone to accuse me of such things. I——"

"Be silent!" The Scarlet Mask had evidently lost temper. The command was roared out in a voice that sounded perilously like that of Leslie Cairns.

Marjorie gave a little amused laugh. She stared straight at the red mask with tantalizing eyes. "Were you speaking to me?" she inquired with a cool discomfiting sweetness that made the eyes looking into hers snap.

"Prisoner, you are insolent." The red mask was careful this time to speak in the earlier hoarse disguised voice.

"I mean to be. It is time to end this farce, I think. So far as treachery, malice and truth are concerned you, not I," Marjorie swept the tense, listening group with an inclusive gesture, "are guilty. Some one of you deliberately wrote me a lying note in order to get me here. Now I am here, but your whole scheme has fallen flat because I am not afraid. You thought I would be. I will say again what I said to a number of you on the campus last March: "How silly you are!"

CHAPTER XXI.

LOOKOUTS REAL AND TRUE.

WHILE Marjorie had gone on to the reception a la masque which had been prepared for her, Jerry had donned her infant costume in a far from happy humor. She could not get over her feeling of resentment against Anna Towne, though she knew it was hardly just. Twice during the progress of her dressing she picked up the note from the chiffonier and re-read it with knitted brows. There was something in the assured style of it that went against the grain.

"Where's Marjorie?" was Ronny's first speech as shortly after seven she flitted into the room looking like a veritable butterfly in her gorgeous black and yellow costume. "I am anxious to see her as a doll. I know she will be simply exquisite."

"She certainly looked sweet," returned Jerry. She paused, eyeing Ronny in mild surprise. Ronny had broken into a hearty laugh. Jerry as an infant was so irresistibly funny. Her chubby figure in the high-waisted tucked and belaced gown and her round face looking out from the fluted lace frills of a close-fitting bonnet made her appear precisely like a large-sized baby.

"Oh, I see. You're laughing at me. Aren't you rude, though? Ma-ma-a-a!" Jerry set up a grieved wail.

"You are a great success, Jeremiah." Ronny continued to laugh as Jerry performed an infantile solo with a white celluloid rattle. "Where is Marjorie? I asked you once but you didn't answer."

"Read that. Marjorie said I was to show it to the Lookouts." Jerry picked up the letter from the chiffonier and handed it to Ronny.

"How unfortunate!" was Ronny's exclamation as she hastily read the note. "When did she leave here? I am glad she put on her costume before she went. She can go straight to the gym, provided she isn't detained over there."

"She left here at five minutes past seven," Jerry answered. "I felt cross about it, too. It seems as though Marjorie is always picked-out to do something for someone just about the time she has planned to have a good time herself."

"What do you suppose has happened to Miss Towne? She was your freshie catch. It's a wonder she didn't ask you to go to her instead of Marjorie."

"Well, she didn't. I have tried to behave like a father to her but she doesn't seem to notice it," Jerry returned humorously. "You see they all gravitate straight to Marjorie. There's something about her that inspires confidence in the breasts of timid freshies."

"She is the dearest girl on earth." Ronny spoke with sudden tenderness. "Are you going out on the campus to parade? I am not particularly anxious to go."

"Then we won't go, for I don't care about it, either." A double rapping on the door sent Jerry scurrying to it. Katherine and Lucy walked in, arms twined about each other's waists. They were a pretty pair of school girls in their short bright gingham dresses, ruffled white aprons and white stockings and tennis shoes. Hair in two braids, broad-brimmed flower-wreathed hats and school knapsacks swinging from the shoulder completed their simple but effective costumes.

They came in for a lively share of approbation from Jerry and Ronny, of whom they were equally admiring in turn. Inquiring for Marjorie, they were shown the note and Jerry again went over the information she had given Ronny.

"That note doesn't sound a bit like Anna Towne," Lucy said in her close-lipped manner as she laid it down. "I know her quite well, for she takes biology and has come to me several times for help. She is awfully proud and tries never to put one to any trouble."

"This may be something that has come upon her so suddenly she hasn't known what to do except to send for Marjorie," hazarded Katherine. "I agree with you, Lucy. It does not sound like her."

Another series of knocks at the door broke in upon the conversation. "Wonder if that's Muriel." Jerry turned to the door. "She may have changed her mind about not letting us know what she was going to mask as."

The door opened. Jerry gave an ejaculation of undiluted surprise. The girl who stood on the thereshold was Anna Towne.

"Come in," Miss Towne." Jerry stepped aside for her unexpected caller to enter. "Have you seen Marjorie?"

"Why, no. I haven't seen anyone except the maid who answered the door. I came over to see if I could go to the masquerade with you girls. Phyllis and a crowd of Silvertons went out to parade. I didn't care about it, so I thought I would come over here."

"Wha-a-t!" Jerry was almost shouting. Ronny, Katherine and Lucy were the picture of blank amazement.

"What's the matter?" Anna Towne flushed

deeply. She did not understand the meaning of
Jerry's loud exclamation. Perhaps she had pre-
sumed in thus breaking in upon the chums.

"Matter! I don't know what's the matter, but
I am going to find out. Read this note. You didn't
write that, now did you?" Jerry thrust the note
into Anna's hands.

The room grew very still as she fastened her
attention upon the communication, supposedly from
herself.

"Of course I never wrote it." Anna looked up
wonderingly. Almost instantly her expression
changed to one of alarm. "There is no one living
at 852 on our street," she asserted. "My landlady
has not moved. I still live at 856. I haven't had
any trouble. I came here dressed for the masquerade. I'm wearing a Kate Greenaway costume. See.
She took the silk scarf from her head disclosing a
Kate Greenaway cap.

"No one living there!" came in a breath of horror from Ronny. It was echoed by the other three
Lookouts. "Then *who* wrote that note and *what*
has happened to Marjorie?"

"I am going to find out pretty suddenly." Jerry
sprang to her dress closet for her fur coat and overshoes. "Go and get ready to go over to that house,
girls. One, two, three, four—We are five strong.
Get your wraps and meet me downstairs. I am

going to see if I can't find Leila and Vera. You had better wait for me here, Miss Towne. I'll be back directly."

Ten minutes later a bevy of white-faced girls met in the lower hall. Leila and Vera were among them. Jerry had met them just in the act of leaving for the gymnasium.

"I'd go for my car but it would take longer to get it than for us to walk. We must make all haste. Now I have an idea of my own about this. I am not far off the truth when I say the Sans are to blame for the whole thing. I would rather think it was they than that the note had been written by some unknown person." Leila's blue eyes were dark with emotion. "And that beloved child trotted blindly off by herself never dreaming that the note was a forgery. Well, I might have done the same."

"I think you are right, Leila. The Sans have planned some kind of seance at that empty house to scare Marjorie. Probably they have dressed up in some hideous fashion. They could easily get away with it on account of the masquerade. The sooner we get there the better. We may be able to catch them, unless they have got hold of her and hustled her off somewhere else." Ronny's voice was not quite steady on the last words.

The seven worried rescuers were now crossing the campus and making for the campus entrance

nearest the direction of Miss Towne's boarding
house. They were swinging along at a pace that
would have done credit to an army detachment on
a hike.

"She wouldn't stand for that. She would fight
every inch of the ground before she would go a step
with that gang." Jerry spoke with a confidence
born of her knowledge of Marjorie.

"They might be too many for her," reminded
Leila. "What's to prevent them from throwing a
shawl or something over her head so that she would
be more or less helpless? I would not put it past
Leslie Cairns."

"They wouldn't dare be rough with her or hurt
her, would they?" questioned Anna Towne.

"No; but this empty house proposition is about
as bad as I would care to tackle. They certainly
have nerve." Jerry's plump features had lost their
infantile expression. Here face was set in lines of
belligerence. She was ready to pitch into the Sans
the minute she caught sight of them.

"This is the street. We are not far from the
house now," informed Anna, as the seven turned
into the humble neighborhood in which her boarding house was located.

"Look!" Jerry, who was leading with Ronny,
stopped and pointed. "There is a *light* in that
house. Let's stop a minute and decide what to do."

"We had better go around to the rear of the house and see if we can't get in by the back door," suggested Vera. "After all, we are only seven in number, and we don't know what awaits us. We are fairly sure that she is in the clutches of the Sans. Even so, they are sure to have the front door locked. They are stupid enough to forget all about the back door. They are not expecting any interference."

"You girls go around to the back. I am going up on the veranda. I shall try the front door. If it is unlocked I will let you know. I'd rather walk in on them that way, if we can. Now for some scouting. Don't make a sound if you can help it, girls. We want to take them by surprise."

Separating from her companions, who stole noiselessly to the shadowy rear of the house, Jerry cautiously invaded the front porch. The shade which had been raised a little when Marjorie had come to the house was now drawn. Still she could see that the room on the right was lighted. With the stealth of a burglar she tried the door. It was locked. She listened at it, then stood up with a triumphant smile. From within she could hear the sound of voices.

As softly as she had stolen up on the porch, she now withdrew. Her feet on the ground, she ran like a deer for the rear of the house. There she beheld dimly a group of figures drawn into a compact bunch near the back steps.

"Front door's locked. How about the back one?" she breathed.

"It's unlocked. Ronny just tried it," Leila whispered. "She says she can open it and go inside without making a sound."

"Of course. She's a great dancer, you know, and light as a feather in stepping. Oh, fudge! You don't know. At least you didn't until I told you. I have given away Ronny's secret. She made us promise not to tell it right after the beauty contest. I don't care. I am glad you know it. I have always wished you and Helen and Vera could see her dance. She is a marvel."

At this juncture Ronny joined them. In the darkness she did not see Leila's Cheshire cat grin, born of Jerry's unintentional betrayal. Leila had often remarked to Marjorie, who had told her of Ronny's concealment of her real identity at Sanford High School, that Veronica was a good deal of a mystery still.

"That you, Jeremiah?" was Ronny's whispered inquiry. "I am going to slip in the back way and find out what is going on. Was the front door locked?"

"Yes; but I could hear voices from where I

stood on the veranda. I couldn't sort 'em out so as to know who was who."

"I'll soon find out whose they are." Ronny shut her lips in sharp determination. "Now for the great venture." Immediately she glided away, and mounted the steps with the noiseless tread of an apparition. The tense watchers heard no sound as she opened the door and stepped inside.

CHAPTER XXII.

THE BITER BITTEN.

For five minutes they waited in silence. It seemed to them much longer than that when, quietly, as she had gone, Ronny re-appeared on the top step of the dingy little porch.

"She's in there," were her first words on reaching the waiting group. "We are just in time to make it interesting for the Sans. Now listen to my plan. What we are to do is this. I have this long black cloak and my mask. It's black too. I am going to scare those girls within an inch of their wretched lives. They are masked and in dominoes. You can imagine what Marjorie went through for a minute. I know a dance called the dance of the vampire bat. It is terribly, *horribly* gruesome. I am going to prance in on them with that. I have danced it in this very cloak. See how full it is." Ronny held up a fold for inspection. "I can make it look like wings. Then with the dance goes a very scary noise, half sigh, half whistle. By that dim candle-

light in there it will be awful. Marjorie won't be
scared. She has seen me dance it.

"The rest of you follow me," Ronny continued
rapidly. "Leila you come first, right behind me.
Stop at the door where you can't be seen from inside
of the front room and line up behind Leila, girls.
Count fifty, Leila, after I am fairly in the room,
then start that awful banshee wail you know how to
give. At the first sound of it I am going to blow
out the candle. Then the Sans are going to take to
the woods. The minute I blow the last candle I
shall grab Marjorie by the hand and flee for the
back door. As soon as Leila has wailed twice every
one of you make the most horrible sound you know
as loudly as you can and hustle for the back door
howling as you go. They will all try to get out the
front door and in the darkness they will have a fine
time of it. If they get a few bumps and scratches
in the dark it will serve them precisely right. What
you must be sure of is to get out of their way the
instant the last candle is put out by yours truly.
The whole thing must be carried out like a flash.
I depend on your support."

"You are a wonder," chuckled Leila. "My stars,
what a party we shall have, with vampire bats, ban-
shees and the like. We shall howl our best for
Beauty. Vera makes a fine banshee, too. Now lead
us on and confusion to the enemy."

Headed by Ronny the rescuing procession stole up the steps. They landed in the kitchen of the house and made their way through it and into the room adjoining which communicated with the short hall on both sides of which the two front rooms were situated.

Due to Leslie Cairns' shrewd business methods the "high tribunal" stood in no fear of interruption. Leslie, finding the house vacant, had rented it of the agent for six months. She had stated that a few of the students intended to fit it up as a private gymnasium. As the agent's mind dwelt only on the glorious fact that he had been handed six months' rental in advance, after charging a rate per month which was three times more than the house was worth. Beyond that he was not interested in the tenants.

The august tribunal had taken pains to lock the front door after them. Due to a squabble among themselves on their arrival at the house, the back door had remained unlocked. Dulcie Vale had been roughly ordered by Leslie to see to it. Dulcie was sulking, however, at Leslie's high-handed manner. She resolved to take her time about it. Then her interest centered on something else, momentarily, and she forgot it.

About the time that the worried rescuers were starting from Wayland Hall, Marjorie was throw-

ing fearless defiance in the faces of her captors.
Her contemptuous arraignment, ending with an
allusion to the affair on the campus of the previous
March, was highly displeasing to her masked listeners. Angry murmurs arose from behind masks
and several sibilant hisses cut the storm-laden air.

"Ssss! Death! Show no mercy!" were some of
the pleasant returns that met Marjorie's ear.

The Scarlet Mask, thus-called, made a sudden
move toward Marjorie as though to lay violent hold
upon her. The other masked figures also took a
step nearer. Marjorie braced herself to meet an
attack, if it came to that. There was a steady light
in her brown eyes which the Scarlet Mask did not
miss seeing. She contented herself with stopping
short directly in front of Marjorie and staring fix-
edly at her. The effect of two malignant eyes peering through the eye-holes of the hideous false face
would have been terrifying to a timid girl. Marjorie was not to be intimidated.

"Prisoner, your remarks are unseemly and ill befit
your serious situation." It was evident the wily
intention of the Scarlet Mask to ignore the guilty
truth which Marjorie had flung at the masked as-
semblage. "You are one against many. It is not
the purpose of the high tribunal to allow you to
escape. You are at our mercy until such time as
we shall choose to release you. You are pleased to

pretend that our identity is known to you. You little know those before whom you now stand. You are in the presence of a group of stern avengers, sworn to see justice done to those whom you have maligned. Were we to remove our masks you would find yourself in the company of strangers. We know you. You do not know us. I warn——"

"Save your warnings, Miss Cairns. I am not in the least interested in them," interrupted Marjorie with dry contempt. "You might be able to make a child of nine years believe you. I doubt even that. I have heard of this foolishness. Malicious as it is intended to be, it is too trivial to be deceiving. You will kindly unlock the front door and let me go."

A subdued chorus of derisive laughter, mingled with hisses arose from the "stern avengers." One of the tallest stepped out from the circle, which they had gradually been forming about Marjorie, and bowed low before the Scarlet Mask.

"I recommend, your highness, that the prisoner be taught at once proper respect for the high tribunal of the Scarlet Mask." The request was made in a voice that aspired to bass depths. It fell short enough of them for Marjorie to identify it as feminine, although she did not know to whom it belonged. She had had so slight an acquaintance with the Sans from the beginning.

"The prisoner will be taught proper respect immediately," vindictively assured the Scarlet Mask. Up went a scarlet-draped arm in an imperious gesture to a domino directly behind Marjorie.

Like a flash, Marjorie whirled about to guard herself. It was precisely what the Scarlet Mask wished her to do. In the instant she turned the figure nearest the leader whisked something white from the voluminous folds of her domino. Marjorie felt herself being enveloped from head to waist in what seemed to be the heavy open meshes of a veil. It was, in reality, a large piece of fish net. She struggled furiously to free herself from it. While she struggled with two of the figures who were attempting to hold her, a third was busy securing the net in a hard knot at her back. As Marjorie was wearing a fur coat and cap, her attire was sufficiently bulky to prevent the net from being drawn very close. She had taken off her mask the moment she had left the campus behind her, so she could at least breathe without difficulty.

Not content with the indignity they had trickily put upon her, two of the dominoes caught her by the shoulders and began forcing her toward a corner of the room. The others followed, closing in upon the trio, so that the silent, but still wrathfully-struggling prisoner would have no chance to make a sudden dash for the door when released.

The Scarlet Mask, now at the edge of the crowd which hemmed Marjorie in, elbowed a rough way to where she stood.

"How do you like our methods now, prisoner?" was the satirical question. "You are going to leave us *at once,* are you? Why don't you go? 'You will kindly unlock the front door,' etc. Oh, my! Naturally we would be keen on doing so after the pains we took to secure your distinguished attendance here tonight. How very sweet you look behind a veil. Too bad you don't wear one all the time. You would——"

"May it please your highness," interrupted a domino in hollow tones, "the time is going. I would advise that we leave here at once with the prisoner. A ride in the still night air may cool her fevered brain so that when we return with her she will be in a more reasonable mood."

"I am also of that opinion," agreed a second. Several other voices rose in approval of the plan.

The Scarlet Mask turned on them in a hurry. Not only angry at being interrupted in her harassing of the prisoner, she did not propose to take any dictation from her companions.

"Who is running this affair?" she asked in the familar tones of Leslie Cairns, minus her drawl. "This little, puffed-up hypocrite is not going to leave here until she promises to mind her own business hereafter. She is also going to promise not to tell where she has been tonight. She may think she won't, but she will, or spend the rest of the night alone here."

A murmur of dissenting voices at once ascended. Half a dozen dominoes tried to force an opinion upon the Scarlet Mask at once. Eager to be heard, there was small attempt made at disguising voices.

"You idiots!" Leslie rebuked in a rage, when finally able to make herself heard. "Have you no sense? Listen to me." Whereupon she centered her displeased attention on her helpers and berated them roundly for daring to set up an opinion contrary to her own.

The dissenting dominoes were not to be silenced thus easily and a spirited altercation began. There were several of the masked company who were hotly against a punishment such as their leader proposed to visit upon Marjorie. Meanwhile, the cause of the altercation listened to what went on with emotions which were a mingling of wrath and amusement. If she had needed evidence to convince her that her captors were the Sans, she had it now. She knew from Leila that the Sans were noted for quarreling among themselves.

After the violent manner in which she had been jerked into the untenanted house, she had not doubted that she might meet with further rough treatment. She knew that Leslie Cairns was quite apt to go as far as she dared. She resolved to show no fear of her captors. She disliked intensely the idea of hand to hand encounter with them. It was utterly beneath her standards. Still she did not hesitate to warn them that she would defend herself if forced to do so. Once she was free of them she had not decided what she would do, further than that she would set off for the gymnasium post haste. Even before the unmasking her chums would miss her. If only she could reach the dance prior to that!

"S—hh! Keep your voices down!" warned a domino who had taken no part in the ill-natured discussion. "I believe you can be heard clear out in the street."

"Mind your business," snapped the Scarlet Mask. "I pay the rent here. It's nobody's business how much noise we make. Who amounts to a button on this alley? Don't be so cowardly. Even Bean has more nerve than you."

This produced a laugh at "Bean's" expense. Behind her enforced veil Marjorie could not repress a noiseless chuckle. How she wished that someone would hear her captors and come to her assistance. No such thing was likely to happen.

The admonishing domino, hitherto peaceful, now took umbrage. "You can't tell me to mind my own business or call me a coward," she stormily hurled

at the scarlet executive. "You make me exceedingly weary!" Her further candid opinion was not
calculated to flatter.

"What you need is a midnight session here with
Miss Bean," declared the Scarlet Mask, with a
touch of cool purpose which caused the angry domino to flare up afresh.

"Try it, and see what happens to you," was her
instant retort.

"Oh, forget it. I merely said you needed it. I
didn't say you would be left here. You are the last
person I expected would go back on me." This
with intent to mollify.

"Well, you shouldn't have——" The somewhat
placated rebel suddenly paused. "Hark!" She held
up a hand for silence. "I thought I heard a noise."

"Someone going by in the street," the Scarlet
Mask asserted, after listening attentively for a moment. At the ejaculation "Hark!" the eyes of the
other maskers had been directed with one accord to
the door. After a brief interval of uneasy silence
the discussion regarding the prisoner was resumed.

The recently ruffled avenger who had given the
alarm still continued to watch the door. She was
not satisfied with her leader's explanation of the
sound. Thus she was the first to note a shadow fall
athwart the doorway. Her eyes widened with fear

to behold an odd, black, winged shape hover an instant on the threshold, then flit noiselessly into the room. It did not advance on the group collected in one corner of the room. It lurched and dipped toward the windows like a huge sable hawk about to swoop down on a chicken yard.

CHAPTER XXIII.

APPARITION OF THE NIGHT.

"A-H-H-H!" gasped the startled watcher, pointing in horror.

"Wh-h-s-s-ss!" The gruesome apparition uttered a sighing, hissing sound which increased in a weird, half-muffled whistle. Simultaneous with the whistle it darted to the nearest candle, extinguishing it with one whining "Puf-f-f!" With horrid grotesquerie it flapped toward another candle, bent on putting it out.

The hood of the voluminous soft black cape which Ronny was wearing was slightly frilled. She had cunningly adjusted it so as to give her masked features an entirely different effect from that of an ordinary domino and mask. A moment's calm inspection would have assured the hazing party that the uncanny visitant was as human as themselves. Her spectacular entrance coupled with the one domino's fear-stricken alarm, had produced upon the hazers the precise effect Ronny had expected to produce. Too greatly startled to take action, a wild, long-drawn, piercing wailing next set in which was not quieting to the nerves. Nor had it ceased when a second eerie voice took it up in a higher key.

By the dim flare of the one remaining lighted candle, the flapping, swaying shape and its hideous moaning whistle became invested with fresh dread, augmented as it was by that volume of ear-piercing echoing sound. Suddenly the last candle winked out, leaving the dismayed avengers in Stygian darkness. Their sharp cries and frightened exclamations were summarily drowned, however, by a new pandemonium of blood-curdling shrieks and groans which proceeded from the hall. Through the half open door leading into the hall came a menacing shuffle as of countless approaching feet. It was the final touch needed to demoralize the hazers. Forgetful of the two front windows, they bolted with one accord for the door opening into the hall, as nearly as each could locate it in the dark. Had a real enemy been present the hazers would have run straight into the arms of the hostile force. Their one idea was to get out of the house with all speed. As it was they showed a temerity born of panic.

In the midst of the hub-bub, Marjorie had experienced nothing more than a faint stirring of alarm at sight of the bat-like apparition. She knew Ronny

instantly, and, guessing her purpose, prudently drew
far back into the corner.

"Come with me." Marjorie now felt the joy of
a familiar arm across her shoulders. "The window. I just opened it. Quick," breathed Ronny.
"I'll steer you to it. We must get away before they
open the front door. It's locked and they will have
their own troubles unlocking it in the dark."

In a flash the two had crossed the room to the
open window. The moment she had extinguished
the last candle Ronny had flitted to the window and
raised it under cover of the stampede. Through the
fish net which enveloped her Marjorie could see a
little, in spite of the shadow cast by the veranda.

"Can you use your arms enough through that net
to help swing yourself over the sill? It is very
low."

"I can manage," Marjorie softly reassured.

Standing behind her, Ronny gave her chum such
assistance as she could while Marjorie essayed a
swift exit from the room which had lately prisoned
her. The instant she found footing on the veranda,
Ronny followed her. Catching Marjorie by the
arm she said: "Run for the back of the house. I
forgot to tell the girls where to meet us. I think
they will wait for us there."

A few running steps brought them to the rear
of the house. A little group of dark figures hur-

ried forward to meet them. The six girls had got away from the house without trouble.

"All's well," Ronny was smiling in the darkness out of sheer satisfaction. "Let's go at once. We had better cross the next three back yards and come out to the street from between them. Hurry. We haven't a second to lose. We ought not talk until we are on the campus again."

Silently, and with all speed, the elated fugitives put Ronny's advice into practice. Once in the street they proceeded north, putting distance between them and the Sans' rendezvous. It was a trifle farther to the campus by the way they took, but none of them minded that. All were too full of elation over the success of their adventure to think of much else.

"The campus at last!" exclaimed Leila as the rescue party reached the gateway. "Let us stop just inside the gate and untie Beauty. She looks like a veiled Oriental in that rigging." Suiting the action to the word she began on the hard knot at Marjorie's back. "While I work, keep a sharp lookout for the other crowd," she directed. "This knot is no simple affair. What time is it, Lucifer-ous?"

"Fifteen minutes past nine." Lucy held her wrist so that the rays of the arc light over the gate fell directly upon her watch.

"Untied; thank my stars! Some knot!" Leila flipped the undesired net from Marjorie. Rolling it up she tucked it under her arm. "Unmasking is at nine-thirty. Let us be there. We can just make it, and it will puzzle some persons to tell who interrupted them tonight. Our talk will wait until after unmasking. Then we can dodge into one of the side rooms and have it out."

"A fine plan," endorsed Ronny. "We are in luck to get here in time enough for the unmasking."

The others heartily agreeing, the octette again set off in a hurry for the gymnasium. Five minutes afterward they were entering its welcome portal. They were obliged to make a frantic dash for the coat room. Once there, wraps and overshoes were removed with gleeful haste. The belated masqueraders entered the gymnasium just as the last, lingering strains of a waltz were being played. It had hardly died away when the stentorian order "Umask!" was shouted out by a junior through a megaphone.

"Here's where Muriel wins that dinner at Baretti's," declared Jerry ruefully. "I certainly did not walk up to her and say, 'Hello, Muriel.' Wonder where she is? I haven't the least idea what her costume is."

"For the sake of old Ireland!" called Leila, pointing. "Now will you kindly take notice?"

A little shout of laughter burst from the participants in the recent adventure as they obeyed Leila's exclamatory request. Coming toward them at a carefully simulated stride was a handsome young man in evening dress. From his silk opera hat to his patent leather ties he was a most elegant person. He was not a particularly gallant youth, however, for his first words on approaching the mirthful group were:

"Don't, for goodness' sake, ask me to take off my hat. How about that dinner you promised me, Jeremiah?"

"Yes, I *guess* so. Oh, but you are polite! Greet us with your hat on and beg for a dinner invitation. My, my! What are the young men of the present day coming to?" Jerry held up her hands in mock disapproval. "Anyway, you win. Your costume is a dandy. I never would have known you."

"What may your name be, young man?" inquired Leila, her eyes dancing.

"You may call me Mr. Harding. I shall not tell you my first name until I know you better," replied Muriel with an attempt at pompous dignity which ended in a hearty laugh. Setting her high hat on the back of her head she thrust her hands in her pockets and beamed on her friends.

"You look for all the world like a debonair young man," Marjorie said admiringly.

"Thank you. Sorry about my hat. To take it off spoils the masculine effect. My hair is rolled under to look short. My hat keeps it in place. But never mind about me. Where have you girls been? I knew what your costumes were to be, so I watched for you from the minute I got here. Confess; you wore dominos over them so that I wouldn't know you. A number of girls did that on purpose to throw their friends off the track."

"Wrong guess, Muriel. We weren't here at all until about two minutes before the unmasking." Jerry tried to speak carelessly, but could not keep an excited note out of her voice.

"You *weren't?* Honestly?" Muriel showed bewildered surprise. "You weren't in dominos? Then where were you? Something's happened. I can read that in your faces." She glanced almost challengingly about the half circle.

"Something happened, all right enough," replied Jerry with grim emphasis. "Marjorie has been through a real adventure tonight. She's been hazed by the Sans and rescued by the Lookouts and a few more good scouts."

CHAPTER XXIV.

AFTER THE FRAY.

CLOSETED in one of the small rooms off the gymnasium, rescuers and rescued told their separate tales of what had happened that evening. Muriel was the only other girl at the private session they held. She heartily mourned the fact that she had not been with her chums. Even the glories of parading about in masculine attire faded beside the evening's adventure.

"What are you going to do about it, Beauty?" Leila asked almost sharply, when the affair had been thoroughly gone over from both standpoints. Dressed as Finestra, a Celtic witch woman, Leila made a striking figure in her white and green robes as she sat on the low wall bench, hands loosely clasped over one knee, her vivid features alive with disapproval.

"I don't know. Nothing, I guess." Marjorie smiled into Leila's moody face. "It will scare them worse just to leave them in doubt as to whether or not they will be called to account. I can't prove that those dominos were the Sans, for I didn't see their faces. Of course, if I accused them of hazing me, in making a report to President Matthews, they would probably be summoned and put through an inquiry. In that case some of them would be certain to weaken and confess."

"True," Leila nodded. "Dr. Matthews would be hard on them. He is so bitterly opposed to hazing. It would stir up a great commotion. They would be expelled. They ought to be," she added with force.

"Certainly they ought," concurred Jerry, "but who cares to be the one to report 'em? I was thinking out the whole thing when we made our get-away from that house. They don't know and they are never going to, unless we tell them, who Ronny was or who did the howling. When they experience a return of brains, for they certainly were rattled, they will naturally guess that the surprise came from students. What they won't be able to figure out is whether they were hazed by another crowd or by Marjorie's supporters."

"They couldn't be sure that Marjorie would not leave word with some of us as to where she was going," put in Lucy, "even though someone did put that line in the letter asking her not to mention it."

"They must have had high ideas of her sense of honor," smiled Vera.

"I felt queer about telling the Lookouts, yet I believed it fair," Marjorie said quietly. "I am glad I did. And now let's forget it and go and have a good time. We really ought to enjoy ourselves hugely, for I doubt whether a single Sans will appear on the scene tonight. If they do it will be late. I hope none of them were hurt in the dark," she added charitably.

"Their fault if they were." Leila rose, her brooding face lighting suddenly. "You have a most forgiving heart, Beauty. As for myself, a few sound bumps will do them no harm. Make no mistake. Those of the Sans who are presentable," she smiled broadly, "will get here as soon as they can. All of them absent would be a grand exposé. Some must appear to take the curse off the wounded."

At that very moment the members of the high tribunal of the Scarlet Mask were engaged in trying to make themselves presentable enough to attend the dance. A crestfallen and weary company of avengers, they had at last made harbor at Wayland Hall. Miss Remson had retired early on account of a severe cold. The dance having claimed the other residents of the Hall, there was no one to mark the line of dominos which stole cat-footed up the stairs. There was considerable repairing to be done both to persons and costumes before the Sans could appear in college society. In that mad scramble to leave the dingy house, which Leslie Cairns had rented with so much satisfaction, there had been casualties.

Natalie Weyman's cheek bore a long disfiguring scratch, caused from a too near contact with a fancy pin or ornament. A jab from someone's elbow had decorated Dulcie Vale with a black eye. Leslie Cairns, who had essayed to unlock the front door in the dark, declared resentfully that she had received more kicks, thumps and bruises than all the others had put together. Due to the fact that the whole party had worn flat-heeled, black leather slippers, which had been purchased in the men's department of a Hamilton shoe store, the casualties were less serious. Leslie had insisted on this measure as a further means of disguising their sex. The hazers had worn their masquerade costumes under their dominos, having been told by Leslie that they would not be more than an hour at the untenanted house. They could easily drop into the Hall and change slippers on their return. It had been Leslie's private intention to leave Marjorie there all night. Joan Myers, Natalie Weyman and Dulcie Vale knew this. The others did not. Hence the objections which had arisen, resulting in the quarrel that had been their undoing.

There was not one of the hazing party who had entirely escaped injury. Tender toes had been trampled upon, jarring jolts administered, and scratches and bruises distributed *ad libitum*. Leslie was outwardly morose. Her inner emotions were too complex to be analyzed. They were a mixture of hate, fear, baffled pride and humiliation. The cherished scheme, concocted by her in the autumn, and on which she had spent so much time and money, had utterly fallen through. Exposure and disgrace stared herself and her companions in the face. Had not Marjorie contemptuously called her by name? While she could not prove her surmise, she could report the Sans on suspicion to Doctor Matthews.

Now that it was all over, Leslie realized bitterly that she and her companions had behaved like a flock of demoralized geese. She had been as badly startled as the others by the appearance of the bat-like figure. She had recently read a very horrible tale entitled "The Bat Girl." It had haunted her for several nights after the reading. Ronny's clever imitation of a huge bat had momentarily paralyzed her with fear. The unearthly shrieks, wails and moans had also served the purpose of the invaders.

Leslie sullenly wished her own plan had been half as well carried out. It was all the fault of her pals. They were always disagreeing. They never worked together. They never exhibited good sense in an emergency. Leslie decided that they should bear the blame for the fiasco. They would hear from her in scathing terms when she felt equal to upbraiding them.

She had been the first one to reach the front door. Feeling for the key, which was in the lock, she had fumbled it and dropped it on the floor. As she had stooped to pick it up, she had been knocked to her knees by the onrush of the others. Callously, she had struck right and left for room to get to her feet. The key had remained on the floor. Knowing that she could not secure it until the wild onslaught on the door had stopped, she had tried frantically to make herself heard above the hubbub. It was of on use.

Presently the panic-stricken Sans had begun to understand her hoarsely-shouted words: "Stand still. The key's dropped to the floor." By that time the wails of the invaders had ceased and their footsteps had died out. An odd silence had suddenly descended upon the Sans. Very meekly they had obeyed Leslie's rude order, "Get out of my way," as she had turned on a small flashlight and located the key. The door opened at last, not a word had been spoken as the dominoed procession filed out into the starry night. Leslie had stepped out first. Stationing herself on the veranda, she had counted them as they passed, to be sure none were missing. "Save your talking until you get to the Hall," she had curtly commanded. "Down the street and hustle for the campus. Keep together."

Bruised and sore, the avengers had again obeyed her without much protest. Dulcie Vale had attempted a belligerent remark but had been promptly silenced by: "You had better keep still. You are the person who claimed she locked the back door. If so, how, then, did that mob of freaks get in? I don't believe they had a key."

Leslie had not condescended to speak again until they had reached the Hall. At the foot of the drive she had halted her party and given them further curt orders as to their manner of procedure. Her final instruction had been: "Get ready for the dance, then come to my room. Wear evening coats. It is too late for dominos now. The unmasking is over long ago. If you're asked any questions simply say we had a dinner engagement before the dance; that we thought it fun to dress in costume but did not care to mask. Now remember, that *goes*."

It was half-past ten o'clock before the entire

eighteen gathered in Leslie's room. Both Natalie's and Dulcie's facial disfigurements were such as to prevent their attendance of the dance. Leslie laughed outright at sight of Dulcie. "You *are* pretty," she jeered. Dulcie's wrath rose, but she swallowed it. She did not care to be taxed further about the trust she had betrayed. Margaret Wayne had twisted her right ankle almost to the point of sprain. Harriet Stephens had a lump on her forehead, caused by a forcible collision with the wall. Eleanor Ray limped slightly from having her toes stepped on. These five declined stoutly to leave the Hall again that night.

"You can't very well go; that's flat," Leslie agreed. "I ought to stay here, too. See that." She turned her back, displaying a large discoloration on one shoulder about two inches above the low-cut bodice of the old gold satin evening gown she wore. She had not troubled herself to dress in costume. "That's what happened to me when you girls knocked me down and tried to walk on me. It is up to me to go over to the gym. I'll wear a gold lace scarf I have. This will hide this bruise. All of you who look like something had better go with me. I don't know what Bean will do. No matter what she tells or how far she goes, you girls are to deny to the end that you were at that house tonight. No one saw our faces. Who, then is going to say, positively, that she saw us, either at that house or on the campus? If we all say we were *not* the ones who hazed Bean, *and stick to it,* I defy the whole college to prove it against us."

CHAPTER XXV.

THE BITTERNESS OF DEFEAT.

WHAT "Bean" intended to do in the matter of
her recent hazing was a question which worried the
Sans considerably during the next few days. The
very fact that they had escaped, thus far, without
even having been quizzed by any of the students regarding that fateful evening puzzled them. True,
they suspected Marjorie's four chums and Leila and
Vera as having been among those who broke up the
hazing party. They cherished an erroneous belief,
however, that there were at least fifteen or twenty
of the invaders.

It was gall and wormwood to those of the Sans
who attended the dance in its closing hour to see
Marjorie, radiantly pretty, enjoying herself as
though she had never been through a trying experience only three hours before. By common consent the rescue party, as well as Marjorie, paid no
more attention to the Sans than if they had not
been present. The dance had been such an unusu-

ally pleasant affair! More than one girl remarked early in the evening to her closest friends that things went along so much better when a certain clique of girls were absent. The Sans' junior classmates were not pleased at their late attendance of the masquerade. They criticized the Sans as selfish and lacking in proper class spirit. Thus the Sans fashioned a new rod that night for their backs of which they were destined later to feel the sting.

The day following the masquerade the sophomore team sent the junior team an acceptance of their challenge. This mystified the Sans five even more. Under the circumstances they had expected and even hoped their challenge would be declined. A refusal on the part of the sophomore team to play them would give them an opportunity to intimate that their opponents were afraid to meet them for fear of being beaten. Deep in their hearts the Sans five were the real cowards. They dreaded playing against Marjorie and Muriel in particular. As Leslie gloomily said to Natalie, "Bean and that Harding snip will certainly get back at you if they can. I imagine Robina Page was one of that crowd who gave us the run."

Leslie had been terribly out of sorts since the failure of her plot. She did not know where she stood at Hamilton as regarded safety. She was

highly disgruntled by the lack of cordiality shown
her and her chums by many students whom she
had considered friendly to her. It was being forced
upon her, little by little, that the Sans were losing
ground. They had sworn to win back their lost
power of the previous year. They had not done
this. Now the game with the sophomores must be
played and she was not in the mood to coach her
team, nor were they in the mood to play. She
doubted if they would dare make use of "the soft
talk." The freshman team had expressed themselves quite openly on that subject about the campus.
When taxed with it once or twice by juniors who
had learned of it and deferred judgment, Leslie had
replied with sarcastic bravado that the freshies had
evidently "heard things" during the game which
no one else heard.

The game being scheduled for the twenty-seventh
of February, Leslie allowed her bruised and shaken
team three days' rest. After that time she fairly
drove them to private practice. She pestered Ramsey, the coach, for new and sure methods of winning points from an antagonist until he resolved
within himself to "beat it" for New York on the
day of the game and leave no address. He had
received a lump sum in advance for his coaching,
so he had no scruples about deserting the ship.

Her five satellites complained bitterly at having to practice every day. All of them had received warnings in one subject or another and needed their time for study. Leslie was adamant. "Just this one game," she said over and over again. "After that we will settle down to work. I am not doing as well as I ought in my subjects. But you must play the sophs and beat them if you can. Don't try any of those new stunts Ramsey showed you unless you can put them over so cleverly no one will know the difference. You will have to be careful. You have a touchy proposition to tackle."

Alarmed at the gradual decrease in their own popularity, the Sans five practiced assiduously during the week preceding the game. They hoped to make a good showing on their own merits. The coach glibly assured them that they were doing wonderful work with the ball. Toward the last of their practice they began to believe it themselves.

They continued to believe thus until after the first five minutes of the game on the following Saturday. With the gymnasium filled by a clamorous aggregation of students, the toss-up was made and the game begun. The sophomore five took the lead from the first and put the Sans five through a pace that made them fairly gasp. All thought of cheating abandoned, they fought desperately to score.

They were not allowed to make a single point. Behind the resolution of the sophs to win they demonstrated a peculiarly personal antagonistic force which their opponents felt, dimly at first, keenly afterward. It was the fastest game that had been played for many a year at Hamilton and it ended in a complete whitewash for the juniors. They retired from the floor too utterly vanquished to do other than indulge in a dismal cry in concert once the door of their dressing room had closed upon them.

Thus Leslie found them. Signally discouraged, she experienced a momentary desire to cry with them. She fought it down, gruffly advising her chums not to cry their eyes out in case they might need them later.

"Don't be so simple," was her barren consolation. "You don't see me bathed in salt weeps, do you? No, sir. Forget basket ball. I swear I'll never have anything more to do with it. I'll send that Ramsey packing tomorrow. From now on, I'm going to keep up in my classes and after classes enjoy myself. If we can't run the college *now*, that's no sign we never will. We can be exclusive. There are enough of us to do that. I don't believe Bean and her crowd are going to tell any

tales on us. For the rest of the year we'll just
amuse ourselves in our own way."

"It's almost a year since we started to rag Miss
Dean and had so much trouble over that affair,"
half-sobbed Dulcie Vale. "You are always making
plans to get even with someone you don't like,
Leslie Cairns, and dragging us into them. You
never win. You always get the worst of it. I
don't intend to go into any more such schemes with
you. My father said if ever I was expelled from
college he would make me take a position in his
office. Think of that!" Dulcie's voice rose to a
scream.

"He did? Well, don't tell everybody in the gym
about it," Leslie advised, then laughed. Her
laughter was echoed in quavering fashion by the
other weepers. Under their false and petty ideas
of life there was still so much of the eagerness of
girlhood to be liked, to succeed and to be happy.
Only they were obstinately traveling the wrong
road in search of it.

Out in the gymnasium the winning team were
being carried about the great room on the shoulders
of admiring and noisy fans. Marjorie smiled to
herself as she reflected that this was a pleasant ending of her basket ball days. She had firmly determined not to play during the next year. Standing

among her teammates afterward, surrounded by a circle of enthusiastic fans, it was borne upon her that she knew a great many Hamilton girls. She had not thought her friendly acquaintances among them so large.

"You did what Muriel said you folks would do," Jerry exulted, when, congratulations over, Muriel and Marjorie were free to join their chums. "You laid the junies up for the winter. That team must have been crazy to challenge you. They played well, for them. Against your five—good night! A whitewash! Think of it!"

"They deserved it." Marjorie's eyes lost their smiling light. The curves of her red lips straightened a trifle. "We paid them for ragging the freshies. They have had two hard defeats inside of two weeks. They ought to retire on them. They are lucky in that we haven't made trouble for them. Between you and me, Jeremiah, the Sans are not gaining an inch at Hamilton. The juniors are peeved with them for not taking proper interest in the Valentine dance. Many of the seniors disapprove of them, particularly since the game they won dishonestly from the freshies. Only a handful of the sophs cling to them. The freshies—I don't know. They are still about half Sans-bound. Just the same, democracy at Hamilton isn't on the wane. It's on the gain."

CHAPTER XXVI.

ON MAY-DAY NIGHT.

THE whitewashing which the sophomore team gave the Sans five, who had so illy represented the juniors at basket ball, was a defeat the Sans found hard to endure. Adopting Leslie's advice, they carried their heads high and affected great exclusiveness. They also entered upon a career of lavish expenditure within their own circle calculated to attract and impress those who had formerly shown respect for them and their money. It was successful in a measure. They could be snobbish without trying. Nevertheless, they knew they had lost irretrievably. The backbone of their pernicious influence was broken.

A warm and early spring brought the basket-ball season to a close sooner than usual. Despite Marjorie's resolve not to play again, she took part in one more game against the freshman. The sophs won by four points, but the freshies were such a gallant five, they came in for almost an equal

amount of applause. They were dear to the hearts
of the sports-loving element of students.

As spring advanced with her thousand soft airs
and graces, it seemed to Marjorie that a new era
of good feeling had come to Hamilton College.

"College is nearer my ideal of it than it used to
be," she said to Jerry one bright afternoon in late
April, as the two stood on the steps of the Hall
waiting for Helen, Leila and Vera, who had gone
to the garage for Leila's car. The five girls were
going to Hamilton on a shopping expedition. The
first of May at hand, the Lookouts and their inti-
mates were going to follow the old custom of hanging May baskets. Leila had proposed it. The
others had hailed the idea with avidity.

"Mine, too," nodded Jerry. "When first we
came back here we thought we would have to depend on our own little crowd for our good times.
Now we have more invitations than we can accept.
It's the same with lots of the other girls, too.
There's a really friendly spirit abroad on the
campus. The day of democracy is at hand."

"I hope so. Anyway, things are pleasanter here
than when we enrolled. Of course, we know many
of the students now. That makes a difference.
Still, there isn't the same chill in the social atmosphere that there used to be. Here comes our good

old chauffeur, Leila Greatheart. She has been obliging and unselfish enough with us all to deserve a carload of May baskets. How many are you going to hang, Jeremiah?"

"About a dozen, more or less," Jerry replied indefinitely. "I'll see how expert I shall be at making them."

"I'm going to make Leila a green one and fill it with pistachio bars and green and white candies. On top I'll put a green and gold lace pin I bought yesterday in Hamilton. I'll make Vera a pale pink one and fill it with French bon-bons. I shall give her a very beautiful string of coral beads that Captain gave me long ago. Vera and Leila have both been so dear about taking us around in their cars, I want to make them special presents. The other baskets I shall just fill with candy or flowers."

"We'll have to make a trip to the florist's late on May-day afternoon or our posies won't be fresh to put in the baskets. I shall buy some little fancy baskets if I can find them. My own handiwork may not turn out very well." Jerry had prudently decided to be on the safe side.

Filled with the goodwill attending the pretty spring-time custom, it was a merry band of shoppers that invaded the Hamilton stores in search of materials for baskets. Crêpe paper, ribbon, fancy

silk and bright artificial wreaths and boutennieres
shown in the millinery windows were purchased in
profusion. Dainty baskets were not so easy to obtain. The girls finally found the sizes and shapes
they desired at the florist's where they placed their
order for May-day blossoms. The confectionery
they decided to leave until the day before the basket
hanging, so that it would be perfectly fresh. "Don't
insult your friends by handing 'em stale candy," was
Jerry's advice.

For four evenings following the first shopping
trip, a round of gaieties went on in one or another
of the basket-makers' rooms. Under their clever
fingers the May-time tributes were fashioned rapidly and well. Even Jerry found she could do
amazing wonders with crêpe paper ribbon and
pasteboard, once she had "got the hang of the
thing."

The hardest problem which confronted the givers
was how to hang their offerings and slip away
before the recipient opened her door and nabbed the
stealthy donor. As there was only one door knob
to each door, the gift baskets must perforce be set
in a row before it. Each girl had private dark intent of smashing the ten-thirty rule and creeping
out into the hall after lights were out. This would
prevent any attempt on the part of jokers to sur-
reptitiously confiscate the fruits of their industry.

Marjorie was confronted by a considerably harder problem. She had a basket to hang which was destined to grace a door quite outside of the Hall. She had purchased a particularly beautiful little willow basket. Through its open work she had run pale violet satin ribbon. A huge bow and long streamers of wider ribbon decorated the handle. The basket was to be filled with long-stemmed single violets which grew in profusion at the north end of the campus. To the curious questions of her chums regarding the lucky recipient of the basket, she merely replied with a laughing shake of her head, "Maybe I'll tell you someday."

When the first pale stars of May-day evening appeared, Marjorie took her violet basket and promptly disappeared. Wearing a plain blue serge coat, a dark sports hat pulled well down over her curls, she crossed the campus at a gentle run and hurried through the west entrance to the highway. Her flower tribute she had covered with a wide black silk scarf. Along the road toward Hamilton Estates she sped, keeping well out of the way of passing automobiles. Onward she went until she reached the gates of Hamilton Arms. She drew a soft breath of satisfaction as she saw that they stood open. She had noticed they were always a little ajar in the day time. She had feared that they might be closed at night.

Seized by a sudden spasm of timidity, she stood still for an instant, listening and peering ahead into the shadows. Then with a gurgling laugh, indicative of her pleasure in the secret expedition, she passed into the grounds and ran noiselessly toward the house at her best speed.

One thing was ecrtain, she told herself, as her feet touched the bottom step of the front veranda, if her presence were discovered there would be no disgrace attached to the apprehension. Her heart was thumping out a lively tattoo however, as she stole up to the heavy double doors and felt for the knocker. There was a light in the hall and in the room at the left of it. Miss Susanna was surely at home. Her hand closing at last upon the object of her search, she stooped and carefully set her basket on the stone threshold. Applying her young strength to the knocker, she waited only to hear it sound inside, then darted for the drive. While she dared not stop to look back, she thought she heard the creak of an opening door when she was half-way down the drive. Slightly winded from her mad dash, she paused outside the gate, flushed and triumphant. Whether the door had opened or not, she had at least succeeded in doing what she had set out to do.

CHAPTER XXVII.

CONCLUSION.

Miss Susanna Hamilton was not the only one to receive an overwhelming surprise that night. Opening the door of her room Marjorie found it dark. With a sharp exclamation she groped for the wall button and flashed on the light. Sheer amazement held her in leash for a moment. The first thing upon which her gaze became fixed was a huge white banner tacked above her couch bed. It bore in large red lettering the legend, "Merry May-day to Marjorie Dean, Marvelous Manager." On the bed, covering it completely, was an array of May baskets that made her gasp. There they were, the very ones she had admired most when her friends were making them.

A trifle dazed at her sudden good fortune, Marjorie stood in rapt contemplation of her friends' tributes. Before she had time to go nearer to examine them, sounds of stifled laughter informed her that she was not alone.

"You may just come out of those dress closets, everyone of you," she called, a tiny catch in her voice. "I know perfectly well that's where you are."

Silence followed her command. Suddenly a louder burst of laughter greeted her ears. From the closets on both sides of the room her chums emerged, fairly tumbling over one another.

"If you will go out by yourself on secret basket-hangings you must expect things to happen while you're gone," Jerry playfully upbraided.

"I never dreamed of any such lovely surprise." Marjorie looked almost distressed. "And I was so mean to my little pals. I wouldn't tell 'em who my violet May basket was for. You shouldn't have taken all this trouble for me, dear children. I'm not worth one little bit of it."

"Go tell that to the second cousin of your grandmother's great aunt," was Leila's refreshing response. "We all have good taste. Don't belittle it. Since you feel a wee bit conscience-stricken over the violet basket, you may square yourself by telling us who it was for."

"I can guess," boasted Muriel. "It was for Miss Humphrey."

"No." Marjorie shook her head.

"Then I don't know; unless it was for Doctor

Matthews," Muriel essayed with an innocent air. "You have a speaking acquaintance with him, I believe."

A shout of mirth followed this ingenuous guess. "Don't guess again," Marjorie implored.

"I won't. I've guessed wrongly both times. I don't know anyone else who might be in line for that scrumptious basket."

"I know where it went, but I'll let Marjorie tell you," Jerry said calmly. "I told the girls they would have time to fix up the surprise before you came back. Vera did that lettering on one of her sheets in about five minutes. Maybe we didn't hustle, though. She had now turned to Marjorie. "Do you believe I know where you were?"

Marjorie looked into Jerry's eyes and smiled. "Yes, I think you know," she answered. "I'm going to tell you all." She swept her friends with affectionate eyes. "That basket was for Miss Susanna. I ran all the way to Hamilton Arms with it. I was a little afraid of getting caught by the servants, but I didn't meet a soul inside the gate."

It was her friends' turn to be astonished. A round of exclamatory remarks went up at the information, followed by eager questions.

"I can't explain why I did it," Marjorie began when the commotion had subsided. "I thought of

Miss Susanna when first we planned to hang May baskets. I felt as though she needed one. She will never know who hung it. I hope it makes her happy. What *I* didn't expect was *this*." She pointed to her own wealth."

"We felt sorry for you in your lonely old age," giggled Helen. "We thought you needed something to cheer you up. But we're not going to hang around here all evening. We are going to give Miss Remson a May shower. Get the basket you made for her and come along. This is my party. I've ordered Nesselrode pudding and French cakes from the Colonial. Think of that!"

"Wonderful!" Marjorie's eyes were dancing. "She will be so delighted to have a surprise party. *She* really deserves one."

"So she does, and so did you, and you have had one." Helen dropped a friendly arm over Marjorie's shoulder. Shyly she endeavored to convey an affection she could not put into words. It was a warmth of regard which Marjorie drew from those who had learned to know the fine sweetness of her disposition.

"I think we are the only ones at Hamilton to hang May baskets," Vera observed. "It's a custom that ought to be brought forward."

"It is a beautiful idea." Ronny patted lovingly

the big blue bow on her basket for Miss Remson. She was extremely fond of the good little manager.

"We ought to go in for more of that sort of thing next year," asserted Muriel. "Goodness knows we have had enough friction to entitle us to the peaceful pursuit of pleasant things."

" 'The pursuit of pleasant things.' " repeated Marjorie. "I like to think of that as our outlook for next year. We have had two years of hard fighting for democracy. I wish we might have peace next year and a chance to invest our Alma Mater with new grace, by bringing back to her some of these beautiful customs. As a junior I am going to think a good deal about Hamilton traditions, too, and impress them on others, if I can."

How truly Marjorie carried out her ardent resolution during her third year at Hamilton will be told in "MARJORIE DEAN, COLLEGE JUNIOR."

THE END

Marjorie Dean High School Series

BY PAULINE LESTER

Author of the Famous Marjorie Dean College Series

These are clean, wholesome stories that will be of great interest to all girls of high school age.

All Cloth Bound   **Copyright Titles**

PRICE, 65 CENTS EACH

MARJORIE DEAN, HIGH SCHOOL FRESHMAN

MARJORIE DEAN, HIGH SCHOOL SOPHOMORE

MARJORIE DEAN, HIGH SCHOOL JUNIOR

MARJORIE DEAN, HIGH SCHOOL SENIOR